Anthony Trollope

Victoria and Tasmania

Anthony Trollope

Victoria and Tasmania

ISBN/EAN: 9783337270964

Printed in Europe, USA, Canada, Australia, Japan

Cover: Foto ©Andreas Hilbeck / pixelio.de

More available books at **www.hansebooks.com**

THE
SELECT LIBRARY OF FICTION.

The best, cheapest, and most POPULAR WORKS published, well printed
in clear, readable type, on good paper, and strongly bound.

Co. y.

SELECT LIBRARY OF FICTION.

SELECT LIBRARY OF FICTION.

SELECT LIBRARY OF FICTION.

HALF-A-CROWN VOLUMES,
Picture Boards.

ONE SHILLING VOLUMES.
Picture Boards.

LONDON : CHAPMAN AND HALL, 193 PICCADILLY.

1–75.

VICTORIA AND TASMANIA.

VICTORIA AND TASMANIA.

BY

ANTHONY TROLLOPE,

AUTHOR OF

"SOUTH AUSTRALIA AND WESTERN AUSTRALIA,"
" NEW SOUTH WALES AND QUEENSLAND,"
" NEW ZEALAND."

NEW EDITION.

LONDON:
CHAPMAN AND HALL, 193, PICCADILLY.
1875.

CONTENTS.

VICTORIA.

TASMANIA.

VICTORIA.

VICTORIA.

CHAPTER I.

SEPARATION.

I PROPOSE in this chapter to say a few words as to the treatment which the Australian colonies generally have received and are receiving from the mother country. In the next I will endeavour to trace very shortly the early history of the most populous and most important in the group, and in doing so I will take my facts from a pamphlet lately published by Mr. G. W Rusden, of Melbourne ;— than whom I have found no one better informed on the affairs of Australia generally, and whose information, conveyed in a small compass, is the latest that has been given to us,—bearing date September, 1871.

It may perhaps be right that I should state that Mr. Rusden's pamphlet is dedicated to myself, lest they who are disposed to think that I am here repaying one compliment by another may claim to have "found me out" should they ever happen to have the two books in their hands at the same time. I find it also convenient to allude to the circumstance, in order that I may take this occasion of expressing an opinion as to the future destiny of our Australian colonies, which is specially evoked by a certain passage in Mr. Rusden's dedication. He, a colonist, seems to regard the colonies as an element in England's future glory,—to look upon Victoria, for instance, as one of the gems by which that glory is to be maintained and consum-

mated. I, on the other hand, who am an Englishman, look
upon the colonies as an element, and a very material
element, in the future happiness of Englishmen,—or of men
and women of English origin,—thinking that England's
glory should be left altogether out of the question in any
consideration of the matter. Mr. Rusden speaks of the
revolt of the American colonies having been brought about
by the "wicked folly of Grenville and North," as though
the effects of that revolt were still to be deplored, and
implies that any act tending to the separation of the Australian colonies from the mother country would be tainted
with the same folly and partake of the same wickedness.
It is most remarkable that this should be the aspect in
which the future of these Australian colonies is regarded by
all the best minds among the colonists. One hardly meets
with an exception among educated men of British origin.
The few of this class who entertain feelings and opinions of
an opposite tendency are generally Irishmen, whose immi-
gration has been of a comparatively late date.

I hope that I am not myself dead to England's glory. I
am indeed well aware that my own feeling on the matter—
my own belief in my own country's pre-excellence—is so
near to self-praise, that it should be checked rather than
enforced. But I cannot believe that the homes of millions
of human beings around the world are to be made subject
to any special form of government, or that their mode of
living is to be regulated in any special fashion, because such
may be the form of government and such the fashion of
living adopted by the country from which those millions
have sprung, and whose language those millions speak.
This form of government and this fashion of living may be
the best the world has yet known. I, with my English
idiosyncrasies, do believe that they are so. I believe further,
—that we at home, with the honest, high-spirited, high-
handed, blundering philanthropy which is peculiar to us,
have, in spite of all the abuse which we have lavished upon
ourselves in the matter, done nearly the best that we could
have done with these colonies. But not on that account
can I bring myself to look forward to their being kept as

"gems" in England's "diadem." As long as the national prosperity of the colonies can be advanced by their dependence on England, that dependence England is bound, both morally and politically, to maintain. When the time shall come in which the colonies can serve themselves better by separation than by prolonged adherence, England, I think, should let them go. The difficulty will consist in fixing the time;—but this question of time is one which must be solved mainly by the colonies themselves. It will be for them to declare, as it was for the United States, when that time shall have come. It will be for us to take care that, when the time does come, the work of separation may be effected, not only without hostility, but without acerbating roughness.

"Here is a continent secured," says Mr. Rusden, "as never was continent secured by the genius of one man, for his countrymen to occupy." The one man is Mr. Pitt, to whose policy and firmness in opposing the attempts which were being made at the same time and with the same object by the French government Mr. Rusden attributes the final acquisition by England of Australia. "On the soil of Victoria there stand between seven and eight hundred thousand persons where twenty years ago there stood some seventy thousand. Thus fresh from their native land, are they not bone of their bone and flesh of their flesh to all living Englishmen as fully as if they still stood on English soil? Must it not be the shabbiest of statesmanship either in England or in the colony which would fret away the ties that bind the one to the other?"

Of course it is matter of pride to us Englishmen that there should be so many of our people in Victoria,—and matter of higher pride that there should be some forty millions speaking our language, and living almost entirely by our laws, and in accordance with our fashions, on the continent of North America. We may probably take the language spoken as the truest indication of the influence of nationality and the justest source of national pride. From our little island we have sent forth a people speaking English who are spreading themselves over all the world.

It is a much greater boast than that of ruling dependencies on which the sun never sets. Though none of the English-speaking nations on the farther side of the globe should any longer acknowledge themselves to be dependent on England, it would matter nothing to the happiness of the race, and nothing to the true glory of the nationality,—so long as the numbers increased, and the material prosperity of those numbers. We are very proud of Victoria,—very proud of having colonised a country rich in gold and rich in flocks, and fitted by nature not only to support but to maintain and to increase the energy which is the gift of our race. We hope that the seven or eight hundred thousand may, as years run on, be quickly raised to millions. That they should have increased so rapidly, and been so prosperous in their increase, is to all of us a matter of self-congratulation. Though individually we at home may be less conversant than we ought with the details of Australian affairs, we keep a sufficiently accurate record in our minds of her rising condition among the communities of the world. We know that the Australians are bone of our bone and flesh of our flesh, as fully as though they still stood on English soil. And we know the same of the Americans of the United States,—in spite of the "Alabama" and indirect claims; in spite of rows about the "Trent;" in spite of existing political differences; in spite of hostilities, should there be hostilities; and in spite even of war, should there be war. The grandchildren of our grandfathers are living there in prosperity and freedom, worshipping the God whom we worship, speaking the language which we speak, obeying the laws which we obey, and animated by that resolve to rule themselves, and to be free from the rule of individuals, which they took from our shores, and which is as strong with us as it is with them.

I deny, therefore, altogether the shabbiness of the statesmanship, whether in England or in the colonies, which would,—not fret away,—but gradually dissolve the ties which bind the one to the other. Such statesmanship,— when it exists, for as yet I am not aware that it has existed, —may be wrong, may be premature, may be one-sided, may

indeed possibly be shabby. Of what matter open to statesmanship may not the same be said? But to declare that
the statesmanship must be shabby that shall have the object
of allowing the colonies to start themselves as a separate
people at some future time, is to pronounce an opinion,—
that indeed may be excused by the warm love of country
which it indicates,—but which can never stand an argument.

I am not aware that any British statesman has as yet
entertained the idea of dividing the mother country from
her Australian colonies,—has ever thought that the time has
now come in which he himself might go to work and
arrange the terms of separation. But I imagine that no
British statesman ever employs himself in the affairs of
these colonies without a conviction that, in all that he does,
he should have before his eyes the fact that separation will
come at some future day. It is impossible that any statesman, or any speculator, that any philosopher should foresee
the time. It must depend on the increasing wealth and
the increasing population of the country. Any invention
—if such invention be within the bounds of natural possibility—which should save the wheat crops of the South
Australian colonies from the disease called Red Rust,
would greatly accelerate separation, because it would at
once increase the population and the wealth of the colonies.
Iron has been found, but iron mines have never yet been
properly worked. If this could be done to any great extent,
it would accelerate separation. Increased supplies of copper
and gold will do so ;—the finding of tin will do so ;—success
in making sugar will do so ;—and the exportation of fresh
uncooked meat to Europe, when such exportation becomes
practicable, will do so very materially. Does anybody
believe that a population of twenty millions in Australia
would remain subject to a population of forty millions in
the British Isles? And the former numbers may be reached
as quickly as the latter.

There is very much to be done before the question of
separation can be regarded as one that is imminent, or fit
for the immediate manipulations of statesmanship. Aus-

tralia must be one whole before she can settle herself and take a place among the nations. There must be some federation of the different colonies before separation can be considered. The states must bind themselves together with the united object of making themselves a nation, and the men who now pride themselves on being Victorians, or South Australians, or Queenslanders, must learn to pride themselves on being Australians. At present they are very far from entertaining any such pride. The inhabitant of Melbourne thinks himself to be very much higher than the inhabitant of Sydney, and looks down from a great eminence upon the Tasmanian. In New South Wales there is a desire to maintain the distance between itself and Victoria, —as though a gulf between the two, which could not be passed, would be for its good. Queensland, the youngest daughter of New South Wales, has but little respect for her parent. South Australia thinks herself better than her neighbours because she has never received a convict. There is, no doubt, something of similar jealousy between different groups of states in the American Union;—but there they have learned the strength of union and have preserved it. As Australia becomes older, and as the number of her leading children who are Australian-born becomes greater, as the tendency to lean upon the mother country becomes slighter, the feeling for the newer patriotism will grow up; and with the feeling of Australian pride will grow the conviction that Australia, to be great and strong, should be one.

The first step towards federation will be the union of the colonies for purposes of general taxation. At present the two great sources of public revenue are the customs duties and the sale and lease of public lands. Let the union be as close as it may, the use of the public lands will probably remain in each colony,—to be applied as may best suit its own wants,—but the customs duties, from which by far the greater proportion of the public revenue is derived, may, and no doubt will, be collected under one tariff, by one arrangement, for the joint purposes of the whole group. At present these colonies all stand towards each other as though they

were various nations, with varied interests, and endeavour each to rise on the commercial injuries inflicted
on the others by hostile tariffs. They charge duties on
each other's produce, and are towards each other as
were England and France before Mr. Cobden had made
his treaty. I do not purpose here to fight the battle of
the border duties,—but here, and again hereafter, I must
repeat the opinion, expressed by me in speaking of the other
colonies, that at the present moment the creation of a customs union should be the first duty of any statesman to
whom the interests and well-being of the colonies may be
entrusted.

I look first to a customs union, then to federation, and
then after some interval,—the duration of which I will not
attempt to indicate,—to Separation and Self-control. In this
idea as to the future of the colonies I cannot think that I am
guilty of any shabbiness as an Englishman. And yet the
expression of the accusation in Australia is by no means
confined to the gentleman whose words I have quoted. Had
it been so,—had I not found it general among those whom
I describe as possessing the best minds in the colonies,—I
should probably have contented myself in endeavouring to
defend myself from the charge with the eager arguments to
which private intercourse is open. But I have heard on all
sides accusations of the littleness of England,—and worse
than littleness, of the weakness and infanticide of which
England is guilty, in her desire to repudiate and put away
from her her own children. I have heard it in details and
in generals. England will not pay for this statue, or sub-
scribe for that building; she will not give cannons and
cannon-balls gratis; she has not left the vestige of a company of soldiers in any one of the colonies; she charges a
price for whatever she supplies, and does not always supply
the best articles; when asked for selected emigrants she
selects the dregs of the workhouses. There are these and a
hundred other details which show the heart of a stepmother
rather than of a parent. But the great general accusation is
stronger still. Her statesmen—or at least some of the chief
among them—have declared their opinion that the links

should be broken which bind Australia to the mother country.
In regard to the details the answer is easy enough. The
daughter has had her dowry given to her,—and should now
pay her own way, and is able to do so. It often seems to
be forgotten, in the colonies, that British statesmen cannot
give away English property out of their own munificence.
The colonies have agreed, with willingness, to certain terms,
which certainly for them have not been unprofitable, and
should not now ask for further small gifts. When our boys
and girls are young we expect them to assail us for half-
crowns, and rather like putting our hands in our pockets,
even when we affect to rebuke the frequency of the solicita-
tion; but when our girls are married and have had their
fortunes, or when our sons have been set up in business by
considerable self-sacrifice on the part of us their fathers,
we do not like then to be told that we ought to pay for
new carpets or cases of champagne. As to that general accusation, I think it is founded not on any words spoken
or acts done tending to immediate Separation, but on
words and acts preparatory to Separation when it shall
come.

The mistake I think is in this,—that the colonists allow
themselves to believe that the mother country is repudiating
them because the statesmen want to save themselves trouble,
and because her people desire to avoid expense;—whereas at
home we feel, not a wish to repudiate the colonies, but a conviction that after a while they will repudiate us, and that we are
bound by our duty to them and to ourselves to be ready for the
time when that repudiation shall come. We are called upon
to rule them,—as far as we do rule them,—not for our glory,
but for their happiness. If we keep them, we should keep
them,—not because they add prestige to the name of Great
Britain, not because they are gems in our diadem, not in order
that we may boast that the sun never sets on our dependencies, but because by keeping them we may best assist them in
developing their own resources. And when we part with
them, as part with them we shall, let us do so with neither
smothered jealousy nor open hostility, but with a proud feeling that we are sending a son out into the world able to take

his place among men. That is the halcyon view which I entertain of the closing days of the connection between England and Australia; and I think that it is one which is tainted with no shabbiness, and which should make me subject to no reproof from any colonist.

CHAPTER II.

" The Discovery, Survey, and Settlement of Port Phillip," is the name of the pamphlet to which I have alluded, and to which I shall mainly trust for the facts to be stated in this chapter. In the lines which I shall quote between inverted commas in the early part of this chapter, the reader will understand that I am quoting the words of the author, Mr. Rusden.

In the year 1802, fourteen years after the first actual occupation by the English of New South Wales, the inland sea which we now know as Port Phillip was first discovered by Lieutenant Murray, who had come out from England under Captain Grant in "The Nelson" with the special object of prosecuting Australian discoveries. The name was given by Captain King, the then governor of New South Wales, in honour of Colonel Phillip, the first governor. Captain Flinders, who, in regard to this period of Australian discovery, is Mr. Rusden's great hero, followed Lieutenant Murray after an interval of ten weeks. The French, in their exploration of the southern coast of New Holland, conducted by Captain Baudin, had sailed past the narrow entrance of Port Phillip without noticing it, and had called the whole region in those parts Terre Napoléon. Indeed they afterwards gave an appellation of their own to the harbour, but did not subsequently attempt to establish it. Captain Flinders, whose name is now perhaps better known from the street in Melbourne which bears it than from the deeds which he did and the sufferings which he bore in these dis-

coveries, is the first who has left us any record of his having
landed on the country which we now call Victoria. " At
day dawn,"—says Captain Flinders, as reported by Mr.
Rusden,—" I set off with three of the boat's crew for the
highest part of the back hills, called Station Peak. Our way
was over a low plain where the water appeared frequently to
lodge ; it was covered with small-bladed grass, but almost
destitute of wood, and the soil was clayey and shallow. I left
the ship's name on a scroll of paper deposited on a small
pile of stones upon the top of the peak ; and at three in
the afternoon,—1st May (1802),—reached the tent much
fatigued, having walked more than twenty miles without
finding a drop of water. No runs of fresh water were seen
in my excursion ; but Mr. Charles Grimes, surveyor-general
of New South Wales, afterwards found several, and in particular a small river falling into the northern head of the
port." This small river was the Yarra Yarra, on which the
city of Melbourne is now built,—and such was, in truth, the
first discovery of Victoria.

In 1803 Colonel Collins landed at Port Phillip to form a
penal settlement, intended as a supplemental offshoot to that
then fully established at Port Jackson,—which the world
used to call Botany Bay,—on the eastern shore of the continent ; but he seems to have chosen his site badly, and to
have kept his men close down upon the sea-shore where there
was no fresh water. This attempt at a settlement was made
at Point Nepean, the eastern headland at the mouth of Port
Phillip, and was soon abandoned. The depôt was removed
thence to the mouth of the Derwent, on the opposite island,
and was the commencement of the great penal depôt which
afterwards flourished in Van Diemen's Land,—if an establishment for the custody of convicts may under any circumstances be said to flourish. From the settlement at Point
Nepean some of the convicts escaped, and one of them was
neither retaken, nor did he return, nor did he perish. This
man, named Buckley, lived thirty-two years among the blacks,
forgot his own language, and became as one of them. In 1835
he reappeared, and was found by a party of white men
who then landed at Port Phillip from Van Diemen's Land.

"No effort was made to colonise Port Phillip for many years after 1803." But during all those years explorations from Sydney as a centre were being made into the continent. "In 1817 Oxley, the surveyor-general of New South Wales, had traced the Lachlan River nearly to its junction with the Murrumbidgee, and had therefore nearly approached the present boundary of Victoria, being within 240 miles of the site of Melbourne." In 1824 an expedition was formed under the auspices of Sir Thomas Brisbane, the governor, the object of which was to penetrate through from the known parts of New South Wales, across the rivers and over the mountains, to the southern coast. This expedition was entrusted to Mr. Hamilton Hume, who was joined by Mr. Hovell, two men whose names are well known among those of Australian discoverers. Both these gentlemen were still alive when I was in the colony, and I will not take upon myself to give to either of them the greater credit in the matter, but will content myself with stating that Mr. Rusden is a strong advocate of Mr. Hume's claims. The great Australian river which we know as the Murray was crossed, and was called the Hume, which name it still bears in its upper waters. After many sufferings and great dangers, Hume and Hovell reached Port Phillip overland. It will be understood that hitherto this district had only been touched from the sea-board, and that the very scanty knowledge possessed by Hume and Hovell as to Port Phillip and Western Port was simply that which had resulted from the maritime discoveries of Murray and Flinders. At any rate they had reached the southern coast of that "Terre Napoléon," of which as yet no real possession had been taken on behalf of the British government. Another expedition was then made by sea to Western Port, under Governor Darling's instructions, apparently with the double object of opening a subsidiary convict establishment, and of confirming the claim made by Great Britain to the possession of the country. This was commanded by Captain Wright, accompanied by Mr. Hovell,—and was made in 1826,—at which time also another convict offshoot of the centre establishment at Port Jackson was sent under Major Lockyer to King George's Sound,—the southern part of that colony which we now call Western Australia. This seems also to have been made with the double object of disposing of convicts, and taking possession of the land as against French claims. Major Lockyer had some success, but Captain Wright had none. "The fears of French colonisation evaporated, and Western Port was abandoned, its shores being described as 'scrubby.'"

"At this period," says Mr. Rusden, "John Batman must be introduced upon the scene. Now Mr. John Batman is a very interesting person, and was certainly the first coloniser of the ground on which Melbourne stands. On the 11th of January, 1827, he, conjointly with another energetic settler, addressed the following letter to Governor Darling, from Launceston, in Van Diemen's Land, to which place he had betaken himself from Paramatta, near Sydney, where he was born :—

"SIR,—Understanding that it is your Excellency's intention to establish a permanent settlement at Western Port, and to afford encouragement to respectable persons to settle there, we beg leave most respectfully to solicit at the hands of your Excelleney a grant of land at that place proportionable to the property which we intend to embark. We are in possession of some flocks of sheep highly improved, some of the Merino breed, and some of the pure South Devon; of some pure South Devon cattle imported from England; and also of a fine breed of horses. We propose to ship from this place 1,500 to 2,000 sheep; 30 head of superior cows, oxen, horses, &c., &c., to the value of from £4,000 to £5,000, the whole to be under the personal direction of Mr. Batman, who is a native of New South Wales, who will constantly reside there for the protection of the establishment. Under these circumstances, we are induced to hope your Excelleney will be pleased to grant us a tract of land proporticnable to the sum of money we propose to expend, and also to afford us every encouragement in carrying the proposed object into effect.

"T. J. GELLIBRAND.
"JOHN BATMAN."

This letter is a clear indication of the manner in which it was then presumed that grants of land in the Australian colonies would be made to those who brought with them the means of occupying the land, and that the grants should be made in some proportion to the capital invested. On this application Governor Darling wrote the following curt memorandum, and we may presume that the answer was in accordance with it :—

> "Acknowledge; and inform them that no determination having been come to with respect to the settlement of Western Port, it is not in my power to comply with their request. March 17 (1827.) R. D."

Mr. Batman was rebuffed, and for a time silenced, but his idea of embarking all his fortunes for Port Phillip was never abandoned. Mr. Rusden goes on to describe how South Australia was founded in 1834, owing its birth to the enterprise of Captain Sturt. Of South Australia I shall speak elsewhere. But it may be well to notice here that although the discovery of Port Phillip was very much antecedent to that of the land on which Adelaide now stands, though Victoria had been crossed from north to south before any attempt at exploration had been made in the sister colony farther west, South Australia was an established province, with a company to regulate her proceedings, with a governor and recognised officers of her own, when the first real attempt was being made by any man to earn his bread or to push his fortunes in Victoria. Mr. Batman had meditated the attempt in 1827, but, as we have seen, had been rebuffed. In 1834, however, Mr. Henty, also a settler in the neighbourhood of Launceston, on the opposite island, determined to make a venture, and this he did,—no doubt having heard of John Batman's failure,—without any reference to the government. "Mr. Henty," says Rusden, "shipped off building materials, agricultural implements, and live stock. On 19th of November, 1834, having lost fifteen head of stock on the voyage, the adventurers reached Portland Bay, and on the 6th of December ploughing was commenced; and thus the first unbroken colonisation of Victorian soil dates from the enterprise of Mr. Henty. In a very short time his few head of stock increased to some 7,000 sheep, and 247 cattle, and 25 horses, and continued intercourse was kept up with Launceston." As it happened, Mr. Henty had made good his footing, guided, as we must suppose, only by chance on the happiest point on all the

southern shore. Portland, and Warnambool, to the east of
Portland, are the harbours of that western district of Australia, which was once called Australia Felix, and which is
in many respects the fairest region of the whole continent.
There Mr. Henty lived and prospered,—and there he still
lives and, as I believe, still prospers; but no great town
sprang up on the site which he had chosen, and therefore
his name has not become conspicuous, as perhaps it ought
to have done, among the founders of his country.

We will now return to Mr. Batman, who did become conspicuous. His mind was still full of that opposite shore,
respecting which he had, with a wide ambition but humble
language, made his unavailing petition to the Governor of
New South Wales. " Provoked beyond endurance, Batman
would no longer be debarred from the downs of Iramoo, so
temptingly described by Hume and mapped by Sturt, He
determined to carve out his own way. South Australia was
being occupied, and the occupation was called laudable in
the preamble of an Act of Parliament. Henty had gone to
Portland Bay, and no man had stayed him. Batman would
go to Port Phillip ; and as the New South Wales governor
had not recognised his right to go there, Batman would
make a convention with the rightful and natural ' lords of
the soil.' "

Batman did go over, and did make a convention with the
natives. He landed on Indented Head, on the western
side of the harbour, and tracked out a large district of
country, including the site on which the town of Geelong
now stands, including the Iramoo Downs and the country
called Dutigalla by the natives ; and on a spot a mile or two
north of the present city of Melbourne, he made a treaty
with them, by which he pledged himself to protect them
and to pay them some annual tribute, and by which they
undertook to surrender to him the country which he proposed thus to purchase. Batman had with him the chart
of the country, as drawn by Captain Flinders, and published
by the subsequent explorer, Captain Sturt, and did not
himself profess, as Mr. Rusden points out, to discover, but
simply to occupy the country. But he prepared, or had

prepared for him, a chart of his proposed purchase, which
he sent to the Governor of Van Diemen's Land, from whom
he first endeavoured to obtain government sanction for
what he had done. "The limits of the land purchased by
me," he said, "are defined in the chart, which I have the
honour of transmitting, taken from personal inquiry." In
this chart, of which Mr. Rusden has published a copy, the
land—not on which Melbourne proper now stands, but
which is occupied by Emerald Hill, Sandridge, and other
suburbs of the city—is marked as "reserved for the township, and other public purposes." The site of the city itself
is a part of the tract intended to be used by Batman for
pastoral purposes.

The treaty is a marvellous document,—as being intended
to make good a purchase of land from the aboriginal
savages, in a country as to which Batman had already shown,
by his petition to the Governor of New South Wales, that
he was well aware that the British Crown claimed the
ownership of it. He must have known that it could not
have been operative either on his side or that of the aborigines. It seems that he landed with the treaty in his
pocket,—with the places for the names and distances left
blank, to be filled by him. When so completed it stipulated
that we, "Jaga Jaga, and others,"—the black chiefs of the
tribes,—"do, for ourselves, our heirs and successors, give,
grant, enfeoff, and confirm unto the said John Batman, his
heirs and assigns, all that tract of country situate and being
in Port Phillip, running from the branch of the river at the
top of the Port, about seven miles from the mouth of the
river, forty miles N.E., and from thence west forty miles
across Iramoo Downs, and from thence S.S.W. across
Vilumanata to Geelong harbour at the head of the same,
and containing about 500,000 acres, more or less." So that
Mr. Batman was determined to obtain a goodly estate, if
in this way it might be obtained. It would probably be
difficult to ascertain how many millions of pounds the land
so defined is now worth. This treaty was made in June,
1835. Batman probably never thought that he should be
allowed to take possession of the land, but did think, and

with just ground, that he would not be expelled from it
without compensation, and that by his occupation of it he
would obtain some recognised position. By asking much
he would get something, especially when he adopted a mode
of asking so much more likely to obtain serious attention
than that which he adopted when he wrote to Governor
Darling. Batman, having so far carried out his scheme,
returned to Van Diemen's Land, and applied to the governor
there for his sanction, sending a chart of his new estate.
But the Governor of Van Diemen's Land had no sanction
to give. Port Phillip was not within his jurisdiction, but
was within the jurisdiction of the Governor-General of
New South Wales. And the Governor of Van Diemen's
Land also remarked, that the recognition of Batman's treaty
"would appear to me a departure from the principle upon
which a parliamentary sanction, without reference to the
aborigines, has been given to the settlement of South
Australia, as part of the possessions of the Crown." There
could be no doubt about it. The British Crown had
decided that it owned all Australia, that consequently the
aborigines had nothing to sell, and that, consequently again,
Mr. Batman could purchase nothing from them. Had Mr.
Batman's claim to purchase from the blacks been allowed,
very many such purchases would have been made,—and
some of the purchasers would have been even less scrupulous
in their dimensions than was Mr. Batman. But Mr. Batman
did not stop here. He also applied to the authorities at
home, and expressed a hope that the Crown would "relin-
quish any legal point of constructive right to the land in
question." But the Crown, or rather Lord Glenelg, who
was then Secretary of State for Colonial Affairs, informed
him "that the territory was part of the colony of New
South Wales, and that no title to lands could be acquired
there, except upon the terms presented in Sir R. Bourke's
commission and instruction from the Queen." At this time
Sir R. Bourke was Governor of New South Wales, and was
also Governor-in-Chief over the Governor of Tasmania.

Mr. Batman, though he was the moving spirit in the whole
matter, was only one of an association in regard to the

capital invested. This association at last wound itself up by selling whatever interests it had to two of its own members; and the government allowed to these two gentlemen a sum of £7,000, in liquidation of so much money expended on a legal purchase of lands; and this was done, as is expressed, in consideration " of expenses incurred by them in the first formation of the settlement."

I cannot complete this short record of Mr. Batman's adventures without alluding to Mr. Fawkner, on whose behalf many have claimed the honour of having founded Melbourne;—and who, I believe, was declared to claim it for himself. Mr. Batman had been busy with Jaga Jaga, the native chief, in June, 1835. In October, 1835, Mr. Fawkner landed at Port Phillip,—also from Van Diemen's Land, whence came all the early settlers of Victoria, so that the leading Australian colony may be said to be an offshoot from that island, rather than from New South Wales;—but the party with which he was connected seem to have made their way across in July. They encountered some of Batman's followers, and, after trying various places for a settlement, made their way up Port Phillip, and at last pitched on the present site of Melbourne, and seem to have settled there, not quite in unity with the Batman party, but without direct hostility. Their feuds, such as they were, will hardly interest the reader;—but it is interesting to learn that the situation of the city, and consequently the origin of the colony, was due to the enterprise of these two men, Batman and Fawkner, and of the associations with which their names are connected. In 1836 there arrived H.M.S. " Rattlesnake," bringing with her, as the official head of the new settlement, Captain Lonsdale,—after whom one of the main streets of Melbourne is now named. This seems to have been the first official recognition of the place; and at that time the town—or rather settlement—had been called by the inhabitants Glenelg, after the Colonial Secretary, whom we, who are old, remember as Charles Grant. It was not till the next year that it was named Melbourne, after the then Prime Minister in England.

This was the beginning of Port Phillip; but Victoria did

not even then exist. From its very earliest commencement Port Phillip was a success. It must be remembered that in those days there was no gold, and that this new settlement was not bolstered up by money from home, as was the case with the convict establishments at Sydney, in Van Diemen's Land, and at Moreton Bay. It seems that from the first agriculture, joined with the growth of wool,—not the growth of wool only,—had been the purpose of those who migrated from Launceston to Port Phillip. We are told as regards the first comers that after so many days,—within five days or within six days of their arrival,—the plough had passed through the soil, and that the seed was sown. Australian colonists had become discontented with themselves in that they had not as yet produced wheat for their own use. In New South Wales the effort to do so had failed. In South Australia it was already succeeding. In Victoria the attempt was at once made, and it has progressed with moderate success. The colony has not as yet been able to feed itself. In 1838 the young settlement had all the healthy roughness of youth. Melbourne consisted of a few wooden huts, and, as we are told, looked like an Indian village. There was a wooden church with a bell suspended from a tree. There were two little wooden public-houses. Kangaroos were eaten because mutton was still scarce. Mr. Fawkner, of whom I have spoken, established a news-paper, but it was a newspaper in manuscript, of which I will speak further in a future chapter. In one of these papers there is an advertisement for a ferry between Melbourne and Williamstown, which is now the port of Melbourne. "Parties from Melbourne are requested to raise a smoke and the boat will be at their service as soon as practicable." The stumps of trees still stood in the one or two streets which were already in course of formation. That such should have been the condition of a young town is by no means remark-able; but that it should so lately have been the condition of a city so great as Melbourne now is, I regard as very remarkable. This was in 1838,—a period which to some of us does not seem to be very remote; and now Melbourne is one of the most successful cities on the face of the earth.

"The Port Phillip settlement was not five years old when its inhabitants began to call for separation from New South Wales, and for its establishment as a distinct colony, with equal privileges to those conferred upon Van Diemen's Land in the south and South Australia in the west. A partial answer to their demand was made by the political reform of 1842, which gave a larger area and political institution to the district, and allowed it to send six delegates of its own to the Legislative Council at Sydney." * But such representation as this by no means satisfied the aspiring political idea of the new settlers. It did not suit them to send delegates to Sydney, which they regarded as a place subject altogether to government authority,—slow, conservative, and down-trodden. Such has ever been and still is the idea held in Melbourne and Victoria generally of Sydney and its surroundings. It seems that from the very beginning of its life Melbourne resolved that she would not be subject to Sydney. The agitation was continued down to 1850, taking at last the form of a demand for absolute separation. In those days,—though they are but the other day,—such requests were not granted easily, as they are now. It was thought wise then to grant slowly and with seeming reluctance. But in 1850 the request was granted, and an Act of Parliament was passed making Port Phillip a separate colony. The arrangement commenced on 1st July, 1851, and its present name, Victoria, is said to have been selected by the Queen herself. On that date Victoria became a separate colony, the fifth in chronological order of those which we know together as Australia. New South Wales had been the first, Van Diemen's Land—now Tasmania—the second, Western Australia the third, South Australia the fourth, and now Victoria, soon to become by far the most important, was the youngest.

But its importance did not come from that wealth of pasture and wealth of corn-bearing soil to which the Hentys, Batmans, and Fawkners had looked when they passed over into the land from Tasmania. What might have been the

* "The Story of Our Colonies," by Fox Bourne.

future of Victoria had her success depended on those simple products of the soil, it is useless now to speculate. In growing wheat she could not have competed with South Australia, as her climate is less favourable for the product. In producing wool she could not have competed with New South Wales, as her borders are narrower and her limits confined. In regard to fruits and vegetables she is infinitely inferior to her despised mother, Tasmania. She has no special gifts of fine harbours, an advantage bestowed by nature, which will sometimes compensate evil qualities in other directions. Port Jackson, Hobart Town, and King George's Sound are infinitely better ports than Hobson's Bay, the roadstead at the top of Port Phillip, into which the Yarra River runs, and which forms the port of Williamstown and the harbour of Melbourne ;—for in reaching this haven vessels have to pass the Rip, which bubbles and eddies between the heads which guard the entrance forty miles down from Melbourne. Luckily for the new settlement, they who had founded it had been men of energy, fit for the work in hand, not expecting too much, anxious of course to thrive, but not looking for instant fortunes, prone to work themselves and capable of making others work ; by no means gentlemen in the ordinary sense of the word, but as good a set of colonists as ever were landed on the shores of a new country. Within fifteen years from their start, if we count from the foundation of Melbourne,—or within sixteen from the date of Mr. Henty's arrival at Portland,—they had already caused themselves to be classed as a separate colony, with a governor of their own,—and a parliament of their own, though not a parliament so thoroughly radical in its construction as that which they now possess. There can be but little doubt that without other chances in its favour a colony so founded would not have been the last in the race. But other fortune did attend it, so rich, so attractive, and so magnificent that it has become the very first on the list. No single British colony has ever enjoyed prosperity so great and so rapid as has fallen to the lot of Victoria.

In 1851 gold was struck at Ballaarat or the neighbourhood. It was soon apparent that the entire condition of the colony was changed by the success of the gold-finders, and that Victoria, as she is now and has been since we first began to talk about Melbourne at home as one of the great cities of the earth, was made out of gold. Gold made Melbourne. Gold made the other cities of Victoria. Gold made her railways; gold brought to her the population which demanded and obtained that democratic form of government which is her pride. Gold gave its special value to her soil,—not only or chiefly from its own intrinsic value, not only or chiefly to that soil which contains it,—but to surrounding districts, far and wide, by the increased demand for its product and the increasing population which required it for their homes.

But this success was achieved by no means without a struggle, nor did the good things come without bringing for awhile many ill things in their train. There is this peculiarity in gold, as an object of industry, that the quest of it disturbs all other adjacent industries. It is natural of course that men should seek that work in which they can earn the best wages, and that any new calling offering high pay will to a certain degree derange the supply of labour ordinarily forthcoming for ordinary occupations. But in all other trades than that of gold-seeking, the customary working of commerce soon brings matters to a level. Wages rise a little on one side and fall a little on the other. Skill, and power, and intelligence hold their own, and the disruptions that occur are those of a passing storm. But gold upheaves everything, and its disruptions are those of an earthquake. The workman rushes away from his old allotted task, not to higher wages, not to 3s. a day instead of 2s., or 6s. instead of 5s., but to untold wealth and unlimited splendour,—to an unknown, fabulous, but not the less credited realm of riches. All that he has seen of worldly grandeur, hitherto removed high as the heavens above his head, may with success be his. All that he has dreamed of the luxurious happiness of those whom he has envied seems to be brought within his reach. It seems to him that the affairs of the world generally are to be turned over and reversed, and that thus at last justice is to be done to him

who has hitherto been kept cruelly too near the bottom of
the wheel. His imagination is on fire, and he is unable any
longer to listen to reason. He is no longer capable of doing
a plain day's work for a plain day's wages. There is gold
to be had by lifting it from the earth, and he will be one of
the happy ones to lift it. The presence of gold is a fact.
All the corollaries of the fact might be plain to him also, if
he would open his ears to them,—but, in regard to himself,
he is deaf as an adder to them. That all the world around
him is rushing to the diggings, he can see ;—and he knows
that there are not princely fortunes for them all. In some
rough way he knows that, were there fortunes for them all,
the fortunes would cease to be princely. But "something
tells him,"—as he explains to the friend of his bosom,—
"something tells him" that he is to be the lucky man.
There is a something telling the same lie to every man in
that toil-worn crowd, as with sore feet and heavy burden on
his shoulders he hurries on to the diggings. In truth he has
become a gambler,—and from this time forth a gambler he
will live ; though his true industry, the sweat of his brow,
which will be really productive for the world's good, will
save him from those worst curses which attend a gambler's
career.

Thus it was that men from all this colony and all the
colonies, and that men in crowds from the old mother
country and from other countries, hurried off to Victoria.
The effect upon South Australia, to the west, was so great,
that for a time it was feared that the young settlement
would be depopulated. Farms were abandoned, and sold
for a trifle. Tradesmen shut up their shops. When their
customers had gone to the diggings, what could they do but
follow ? Shepherds from the recently stocked pastures of
the Riverina and the Darling rushed down over the Murray.
And worse still, the shearers who should have shorn the
flocks were gone when the fleeces were ready for the shears.
All these were welcomed by the young colony. There was
no jealousy of new-comers as long as those who came bore
characters as honest men,—or had at least had no brands
upon the forehead. But the convicts from Tasmania broke

loose and swelled the crowd. Barriers which had sufficed to retain the unexcited felon availed nothing when the imagination of the wretch had been inflamed by tidings of gold. They also swarmed over from the island and joined the crowd, to the loudly expressed disgust of a colony which was perhaps somewhat Pharisaical by reason of her own comparative purity.

Then there arose such a turmoil of circumstances, such a hurly-burly of social and material wants, as men were sure not to have anticipated, though in looking back upon the facts every one now can see well that they were unavoidable. How was the crowd to feed itself, to shelter itself, and to clothe itself? With such business as that on which they were engaged, deficiencies in respect of house accommodation could be endured. The smallest and the roughest tents sufficed. Boots, trousers, and a flannel shirt completed the wardrobe of many a high-born digger, and as long as the articles would hold together men working for gold would be content. But there must be food ; and the feeding of 20,000 men, brought together as though by magic, requires almost miraculous energy. All things in the neighbourhood of the diggings became extravagantly dear,—so dear that the absolute value of the article seemed hardly to bear at all on the price fixed. And in response to this, or rather as an encouragement to it, the diggers themselves, with newly found gold in their hands, indifferent as they were to comforts, seemed hardly to care what they paid for those luxuries of which they had dreamed. To such a one it was nothing to give an ounce of gold for a bottle of so-called champagne, though the champagne had cost in Melbourne perhaps 3s. 6d., and the gold was worth certainly more than £3 10s.

But who was to supply the wants of diggers when every one was himself a digger? Or, if there were some steady enough to resist the temptation and to cling to haunts which were comparatively old, how were they to obtain that assistance in their work of living, which in this complex world we all render one to another? Who was to cook his dinner for the unfortunate lawyer who had lately settled in the rising

town of Melbourne, when every young woman had rushed off
to the diggings, to get whatever wages she chose to ask,
even if she could not do better for herself by getting a digger as a husband? Or, whoever was to sell him a mutton
chop to be cooked, when the half-dozen butchers of the
rising metropolis had gone away to the diggings, either
themselves to dig or else to follow the much more profitable
occupation of supplying the diggers? For it was soon found
that this first El Dorado had brought a second with it.
There was already a double set of gold-seekers. It was a
grand thing to drink champagne at an ounce of gold the
bottle; but it was a much better thing, if not a grander, to
sell champagne at that price. It was fine to get a nugget;
—only that nuggets were so uncertain. But there were
nuggets found daily by some happy diggers, and those who
found were always ready to buy everything that was offered
to them. That second El Dorado was more certain though
less glorious than the first.

There was, indeed, an earthquake which at first it seemed
impossible that the community as a whole should withstand.
Everything was disordered and out of place. All that had
been at the bottom was at the top. That which had been
at the top was at the bottom. How were these men to be
governed, who by the very nature of their calling want much
of that protection which we call government? Something of
the same kind occurred in the early days of California,—but
not to the same extent; and there Lynch law had prevailed.
They who saw those times in California declare that society
there was preserved by Lynch law;—that, bad as it must
necessarily be, unjust, tyrannical, cruel, conducive as it must
be to a reign of terror and unlimited power in the hands of
some few utterly unfit to use it, it was infinitely better than
the no-law which would otherwise have prevailed. But California had then been very distant from any recognised seat
of power, whereas Ballaarat was no more than 100 miles
from Melbourne. The government was bound to govern,—
to send magistrates, commissioners, inspectors, constables,
and the like. But you cannot make a man be a constable,
nor even a magistrate, against his will. When the men to

be watched were finding nuggets of gold before noon, and nuggets in the afternoon, and nuggets at night, at what rate per annum and per week were you to pay your magistrates and your constables ?

The reader will not, I think, fail to understand that there was much of what we call rough work in the colony at that time.   There arose one turmoil so loud that soldiers were called on to fight the miners, and that miners entrenched themselves within palisades, intending to fight the soldiers. This, too, occurred at Ballaarat, and I shall say perhaps a word of that affair when speaking of Victoria's mining capital. My present object is to show the conditions through which the colony has passed, and the causes which have made it what it is.   Gradually things settle themselves into the old grooves, and the earthquake died out.   Its rumblings were still heard,—but at last it rumbled only, and did not frighten. And when it had passed away the causes which had created it had filled the land with wealth.   Many had been ruined. Many a youth, who in his own country had enjoyed all that love and education could do for him, had come out to perish miserably in the mud of an Australian gully.   There had been terrible suffering, crushing disappointment,—all the agonies of toil, at first hopeful, but at last utterly unremunerative, of which no history can ever be written.   There had been broken hopes, wasted energies, the ague-fit after the fever.   But a people had been established, and a land had been enriched.   This, I take it, is all that need be said of the early history of Victoria.

CHAPTER III.

MELBOURNE has certainly made a great name for itself, and is the undoubted capital, not only of Victoria but of all Australia. It contains, together with her suburbs, 206,000 souls, and of these so-called suburbs the most populous are as much a part of Melbourne as Southwark is of London ;— or were I to say as Marylebone is of London, my description would be true, as there is no line of demarcation traceable by any eyes but those of town-councillors and the collectors of borough rates. There are very many cities in the world with larger populations,—so many that the number does not strike one with surprise. But I believe that no city has ever attained so great a size with such rapidity. Forty years ago from the present date (1873), the foot of no white man had trodden the ground on which Melbourne now stands, unless it was the foot of Buckley the escaped convict, who lived for thirty years with a tribe of native savages.

Melbourne is not a city beautiful to the eye from the charms of the landscape surrounding it, as are Edinburgh and Bath with us, and as are Sydney and Hobart Town in Australia, and Dunedin in New Zealand. Though it stands on a river which has in itself many qualities of prettiness in streams,—a tortuous, rapid little river with varied banks,— the Yarra Yarra by name, it seems to have but little to do with the city. It furnishes the means of rowing to young men, and waters the Botanical Gardens. But it is not "a joy for ever" to the Melbournites, as the Seine is to the

people of Paris, or the Inn to the people of Innsbruck.
You might live in Melbourne all your life and hardly know
that the Yarra Yarra was running by your door. Nor is
Melbourne made graceful with neighbouring hills. It stands
indeed itself on two hills, and on the valley which separates
them ; and these afford rising ground sufficient to cause considerable delay to the obese and middle-aged pedestrian
when the hot winds are blowing,—as hot winds do blow at
summer-time in Melbourne. But there are no hills to produce scenery, or scenic effect.

Nevertheless the internal appearance of the city is certainly magnificent. The city proper,—that Melbourne itsel
which is subject to the municipal control of the mayor, and
which in regard to all its municipal regulations is distinct
from its suburbs,—is built on the Philadelphian, rectangular,
parallelogrammic plan. Every street runs straight, and every
other street runs either parallel to it or at right angles with
it. The principal streets run east and west,—Great Flinders
Street, then Collins Street,—which is the High Street of the
city, and its Regent Street and Bond Street ; then Bourke
Street,—which is its Oxford Street and Cheapside ; and then
beyond them Latrobe Street, Lonsdale Street, and others.
Second class streets, but streets which do not admit
themselves to be second class, run at right angles to these ;
Russell Street, Swanston Street,—a street which by no means
thinks itself second class ; Elizabeth Street,—also a proud
street ; Queen Street, William Street, and King Street. And
then between all these streets,—which are busy streets,—
there run little streets calling themselves lanes, and assuming
generally the name of their big brother. Thus there are
Flinders Lane and Collins Lane, and so on. But they are
all regular, all rectangular, and all parallelogrammic.

It is the width of the streets chiefly which gives to the city
its appearance of magnificence ;—that, and the devotion of
very large spaces within the city to public gardens. These
gardens are not in themselves well kept. They are not lovely,
as are those of Sydney in a super-excellent degree. Some
of them are profusely ornamented with bad statues. None
of them, whatever may be their botanical value, are good

gardens. But they are large and numerous, and give an air
of wholesomeness and space to the whole city. They afford
green walks to the citizens, and bring much of the health
and some of the pleasures of the country home to them all.

One cannot walk about Melbourne without being struck
by all that has been done for the welfare of the people
generally. There is no squalor to be seen,—though there
are quarters of the town in which the people no doubt are
squalid. In every great congregation of men there will be a
residuum of poverty and filth, let humanity do what she
will to prevent it. In Melbourne there is an Irish quarter,
and there is a Chinese quarter, as to both of which I was
told that the visitor who visited them aright might see much
of the worst side of life. But he who would see such misery
in Melbourne must search for it especially. It will not meet
his eye by chance as it does in London, in Paris, and now
also in New York. The time will come no doubt when it
will do so also in Melbourne, but at present the city, in all
the pride of youthful power, looks as though she were
boasting to herself hourly that she is not as are other cities.

And she certainly does utter many such boasts. I do not
think that I said a pleasant word about the town to any
inhabitant of it during my sojourn there, driven into silence
on the subject by the calls which were made upon me for
praise. " We like to be cracked up, sir," says the American.
I never heard an American say so, but such are the words
which we put into his mouth, and they are true as to his
character. They are equally true as to the Australian generally, as to the Victorian specially, and as to the citizen
of Melbourne in a more especial degree. He likes to be
" cracked up," and he does not hesitate to ask you to
" crack him up." He does not proceed to gouging or bowie
knives if you decline, and therefore I never did crack
him up.

I suppose that a young people falls naturally into the fault
of self-adulation. I must say somewhere, and may as well
say here as elsewhere, that the wonders performed in the way
of riding, driving, fighting, walking, working, drinking, love-
making, and speech-making, which men and women in Australia

told me of themselves, would have been worth recording
in a separate volume had they been related by any but the
heroes and heroines themselves. But, reaching one as they
did always in the first person, these stories were soon received as works of a fine art much cultivated in the colonies,
for which the colonial phrase of " blowing" has been created.
When a gentleman sounds his own trumpet he "blows."
The art is perfectly understood and appreciated among the
people who practise it. Such a gentleman or such a lady
was only "blowing !" You hear it and hear of it every
day. They blow a good deal in Queensland ;—a good deal
in South Australia. They blow even in poor Tasmania.
They blow loudly in New South Wales, and very loudly in
New Zealand. But the blast of the trumpet as heard in
Victoria is louder than all the blasts,—and the Melbourne
blast beats all the other blowing of that proud colony. My
first, my constant, my parting advice to my Australian
cousins is contained in two words—" Don't blow."

But if a man must blow it is well that he should have
something to blow about beyond his own prowess, and I do
not know that a man can have a more rational source of
pride than the well-being of the city in which he lives. It
is impossible for a man to walk the length of Collins Street
up by the churches and the club to the Treasury Chambers,
and then round by the Houses of Parliament away into
Victoria Parade, without being struck by the grandeur of
the dimensions of the town. It is the work of half a morning for an old man to walk the length of some of the streets,
and to a man who cannot walk well the distances of Melbourne soon become very great indeed. There seems to be
this drawback upon noble streets, and large spaces, and
houses with comfortable dimensions, that as the city grows
the distances become immense. They are now far longer
in Melbourne with its 200,000 inhabitants clustered together than in Glasgow with 500,000 ; and as the population
increases and houses are added to houses, it will become
impossible for pedestrians to communicate unless they devote
the entire day to travelling. There will, no doubt, be railways about the town, as there are about London, but it

seems strange that half a million of people should not be
able to live together within reach of each other.

The city, I have said, is magnificent,—and yet no street
in it is finished. Even in Collins Street the houses stand in
gaps. Here and there are grand edifices,—in the first place
banks, as to which it seems that in these days grandeur pays
as in old days did that quiet, almost funereal, deportment
which was the characteristic of Lombard Street, and is still
maintained by one or two highly respectable London firms.
The banks in Melbourne are pre-eminent, and next to them
the warehouses of ambitious retail dealers. And there are
some very handsome churches,—not always built with close
attention to the proprieties of church architecture as recognised by us, but nevertheless handsome. Here and there
is a grand public building,—the Post Office and the Town
Hall being very grand. There are Institutions of various
kinds, all having domiciles more or less magnificent. A
few private houses have been built with architectural pre-
tensions, and in this way there is enough of detailed splendour to give a character to the streets. But no street is
as yet splendid throughout. In speaking of the outward
appearance of Melbourne, I must not forget the gutters,
which in rainy weather run down each side of the street like
little rivers. These are now bridged over so constantly
and so well that they offer practically but little impediment
to the walker. In hot weather they often flow with water
from the reservoir, and help to cool the town. But in the
old days,—when the bridges were few and far between, or
when there were no bridges at all,—it used to be a work of
danger to get about. It was then no uncommon thing to
hear that "another child" had been drowned in Melbourne
that morning.

Though the suburbs of Melbourne,—such specially as
Collingwood, Fitzroy, and Richmond,—are in fact parts of
the town, they seem to have been built on separate plans,
and each to have had a ceremonial act of founding or settlement on its own part,—being in this respect unlike suburbs,
which are usually excrescences upon a town, arising at hap-
hazard as houses are wanted. But these subsidiary towns

D

are all rectangular and parallelogrammic on their own bottom, though not rectangular and parallelogrammic in regard to Melbourne. If the streets of the one run from north to south, and from east to west, the streets of the other run from north-east to south-west, and from south-east to north-west. This seems to have been of importance,—and equally so that they should have separate mayors, separate town-councils, and above all separate town-halls. Collingwood has over 18,000 inhabitants; Emerald Hill over 17,000; Richmond over 16,000; and Fitzroy over 15,000 inhabitants; but to the world at large these places are parts of Melbourne.

But the magnificence of Melbourne is not only external. The city is very proud of its institutions, and is justified in its pride. Foremost among these, as being very excellent in the mode of its administration, is the public Library. In the first place it is open gratuitously to all the world, six days a week, from ten in the morning till ten in the evening. In the second place, whatever the library possesses can be got by any reader without trouble. It contained indeed, in 1870, no more than 60,000 volumes, which to those who are accustomed to wander among the shelves of the British Museum, or of the Oxford and Cambridge libraries, does not seem to be a large number. But the books have been selected for the uses of the people, and in such a library multiplied editions are hardly necessary. And the too vast multiplication of volumes leads to infinite difficulty in the manipulation of them. Here at Melbourne any man who is decent in his dress and behaviour can have books, shelter, warmth, chair, table, and light up to ten at night, day after day, night after night, year after year,—and all for nothing. For women, who choose to be alone,—and in the colonies as in the United States it is always presumed that women will choose to be alone,—a separate room is provided. This is only beaten at Boston, Massachusetts, where the inhabitants of the city are allowed to take the books home with them.

Melbourne also has its University,—which has hardly as yet been as successful as its Library; though for it, as for that at Sydney, I do not doubt that success will be forthcoming. It is at present richer in the possession of council, of senate, of doctors of law and medicine, and in masters of arts, than it is in students. In 1870 seven gentlemen took degrees as bachelors of arts, the average of ten years having been five in each year. In 1870, 122 students, in all, attended lectures,—a number which is poor for a university with a chancellor, a vice-chancellor, a senate, four professors, and nine other lecturers. In 1870 the government paid £9,000 towards the expenses of the University, the college fees amounting to no more than £2,793 ;—a pecuniary result which must be acknowledged to be poor in so rich a community. But in considering all this the nature of the community must be borne in mind, and the fact, that though education generally is more desired by such a people than it is in an old country such as ours, education of a high order is by no means equally in demand. People even who are rich are unwilling to pay the expenses of procuring it for their children,—an expense which is not at all in proportion with their previous experience of the cost of education. It will probably be acknowledged that a government, in such circumstances, is right to support a university among its people till the time shall come in which a class shall have grown up willing to support it for themselves.

The University itself is a modest, pretty quadrangular building, of which three sides are completed, containing simply the lecture-rooms and library, and the residences of the professors. The fourth side will be added as funds are found. The University itself does not profess to provide accommodation for the residence of scholars. Attached to it, however, is an affiliated institution called Trinity College, —got up in the interests of the Church of England, and I believe I shall be correct in saying, chiefly by the energy of that most excellent of men, the present bishop. No salary is here provided by government for a fainéant Head of the House, as I found to be the case at Sydney. When I visited the Melbourne University in 1872, there was Trinity College,*

* I have since been much pleased at learning that the affiliated college was nearly full.

but as yet there were no collegians. The building had been erected and furnished, and was ready to take in twenty students, at 30s. a week for board and lodging. Here, it was hoped, might the future young pastors of the Church of England in the colony receive their learning. Seeing how much had been done by how good a man, I give the new college all my best wishes. Behind the University, and in the grounds belonging to it, stands the Museum, which is open to the public gratuitously. I am not, myself, qualified to speak of the value of museums, but this one seems to have the special and somewhat unusual merit of being so arranged that its contents are intelligible to ordinary capacities.

I have spoken of the gardens of Melbourne generally as contributing largely to the spacious dimensions of the town ; but I must not omit to make special mention of the Botanical Gardens, and of their learned curator, Dr. Von Mueller. Dr. Von Mueller, who is also a baron, a fellow of half the learned societies in Europe, and a Commander of the Order of St. Jago, has made these gardens a perfect paradise of science for those who are given to botany rather than to beauty. I am told that the gardens and the gardener, the botany and the baron, rank very highly indeed in the estimation of those who have devoted themselves to the study of trees, and that Melbourne should consider herself to be rich in having such a man. But the gardens though spacious are not charming, and the lessons which they teach are out of the reach of ninety-nine in every hundred. The baron has sacrificed beauty to science, and the charm of flowers to the production of scarce shrubs, till the higher authorities have interfered. When I was at Melbourne there had arisen a question whether there should not be some second and, alas ! rival head-gardener, so that the people of Melbourne might get some gratification for their money. The quarrel was running high when I was there. I can only hope that flowers may carry the day against the shrubs.

There are no poor-laws in the colonies, and consequently no poor-rates. Destitute men and women are not entitled by law to be fed and housed at the public expense, as they are in England. As far as the law is concerned any man who cannot feed himself may lie down and die. But such is not the result of things as they exist. Poor and destitute there are, though they are very few in number as compared with those among us at home. Work is more plentiful. Wages are higher. Food is cheaper. In his personal condition the working man does not stand always near to the edge of the precipice of destitution, as he too frequently does in Europe. But there are poor,—both men and women,—and for them shelter and food are found, and very many of the comforts of life. These are provided in buildings called Benevolent Asylums, of which there are five in Victoria,— the largest establishment being in Melbourne. Here, in Melbourne, about 12,000 poor are relieved in the course of the year, some using it as a temporary refuge and some living in it altogether. No one is ever turned out; nor does there seem to be any great difficulty in getting in if the applicant be really destitute. It is worthy of remark that a very small proportion of those who apply for relief are colonial born. The growth of the colony, and the fact that most of the aged in the country have been immigrants, will account for this in some degree. But though Victoria is still growing the colonies are old enough to have produced destitution of their own. In 1870 there were 11,739 persons in the Victorian Benevolent Asylums, of which but little more than a tenth were born in the colony. This I attribute to the fact that the generation born in the colonies drinks less and is more careful of its means than they who go thither from Europe. The theory of these asylums is that they should be supported by voluntary contribution with aid from government. The fact is that they are supported by government with some little aid from voluntary contribution,—and with something made by the work of the inmates. In 1870 the asylum at Melbourne cost £18,856, of which £15,000 were paid by the government, and but £2,000 by private contributions. In Victoria government pays for everything; and, why should the benevolent contribute when the thing is provided in a different way? I have said that there were no poor-rates ;—but perhaps it may be thought that the same thing is effected when the parliament makes a grant out of the general taxes of the country. Could a pauper be suddenly removed out of an English union workhouse into the Melbourne Benevolent Asylum, he might probably think that he had migrated to Buckingham Palace.

When giving a catalogue of the peculiar institutions of Melbourne, I must not omit " The Verandah." Not that there is anything beautiful or grand about the Verandah, or that it is an institution of which Melbourne is inclined to boast. It is one, however, which she uses perhaps with more thorough devotion than all the others put together. The opportunities offered by it are never neglected ; and they who have once tasted its charms, seldom fail to return to them. " The Verandah " is a morsel of pavement in Collins Street, on which men congregate under a balcony, and there buy and sell gold shares. It is a small Bourse or " Capel Court," held out of doors, the operations of which are conducted with all the broad daylight of the public street upon them,—but not on that account conducted with any peculiar formality or reticence. I shall, however, be under the necessity of speaking of " The Verandah " again when describing the gold-fields of the colony and the operations which they have produced.

I visited the Lunatic Asylum at Yarra Bend,—or rather the two lunatic asylums, for there is an old and a new establishment on opposite sides of the river Yarra,—and other hospitals, and the penal establishment at Pentridge and other gaols. I could tell how many inmates there were in each, and how much each inmate cost,—no doubt with all that inaccuracy which a confidence in statistics customarily produces. But I doubt whether I should serve or interest any one by doing so. But it may be well to express the general conviction left on my mind by all these visitings,—not only in reference to Melbourne and Victoria, but as regards the colonies generally,—that a care for public things predominates in them all. However greedy individuals may be after the wealth of each other, whatever fall.

ings off there may be in individual morality and honesty,
whatever lapses in individual honour, the care of public
things is maintained throughout with an unspairing expenditure. In nothing is this more conspicuous than in the
protection given to the afflicted by the State. Let the cost
be what it may, the poor are to be taught, the needy
sheltered and fed, and the afflicted, whether in mind or
body, relieved as far as outward appliances may relieve
them.

Melbourne is the centre of a series of railways of which I
shall speak in another chapter, as they belong to the colony
generally rather than to the town; but the city has the
advantage of a local line,—belonging to a private company
and not worked by the government as are the colonial lines
generally,—which passes from St. Kilda and Emerald Hill
on one side, through Melbourne to Richmond, Prahran,
Brighton, and other suburbs on the other side, which is so
generally used that Melbourne itself is nearly as hollow
as London. I may almost say that no one lives in Melbourne. Of this, one consequence is disagreeable. When
you dine out you are generally under the necessity of
returning by railway,—which is an abomination. But in
other respects the railway is a great blessing. People
even of moderate means live in the country air and
have gardens and pleasant houses. On two sides, south
and east, Melbourne is surrounded for miles by villa
residences.

There is now being built, very close to the town, a new
Government House, which is intended to be very magnificent. The governors who occupy it will probably find it
by far too much so. The present house, which is four
miles out of town, is very much abused as being inadequate
to its purpose. It certainly is much less grand than those
at Sydney, at Hobart Town,—which is first among government houses,—or even at Perth in poor Western Australia.
Nevertheless I was present there at a public ball, at which
all Melbourne was entertained with true vice-royal munificence. Were I appointed governor of a colony, I should
deprecate very much a too palatial residence. I think it

may be admitted as a rule that governors find it hard to
live upon the salaries allotted to them, and generally do not
do so. Men used to accept bishopricks and governorships
with a view to making fortunes. It is beginning to be
admitted now that men with private means are wanted for
both.

There is perhaps no town in the world in which an ordinary working man can do better for himself and for his
family with his work than he can at Melbourne. There
may be places at which wages are higher, but then at those
places the necessaries of life are dearer and the comforts of
life less easily attainable. There are others undoubtedly at
which living is cheaper;—but there also are wages lower,
and the means of living less salutary and commodious.
When I left Melbourne in July, 1872, flour was cheaper
than in England. The price of wheat was then 6s. 8d. a
bushel in the Melbourne markets. Meat had risen greatly
during the last twelve months in consequence of the increased exportation and the rise in the price of wool, and
then ranged in the city from 4d. to 6d. the pound. Butter
varied from 6d. to 1s. 9d. the pound; potatoes from £3 to
£4 the ton; eggs from 10d. to 2s. the dozen; tea from
1s. 6d. to 2s. 6d. the pound; coffee from 1s. to 1s. 10d. a
pound; coals from 28s. to 35s. a ton. The price of clothes,
taken all round, is I think about 20 per cent. dearer than in
London. A working man in Melbourne no doubt pays
more for his house or for his lodgings than he would in
London; but then in Melbourne the labourer or artisan
enjoys a home of a better sort than would be within the
reach of his brother in London doing work of the same
nature, and in regard to house-rent gets more for his money
than he would do at home. In Melbourne the wages of
artisans and mechanics generally are 10s. a day. Such is
stated by the registrar of the colony to have been the
customary payment to blacksmiths, carpenters, masons, and
bricklayers in 1870, and I am assured that there has been
no reduction since that date. Gardeners receive from 50s.
to 60s. a week, and common labourers about 36s. a week.
These men, so paid, are supposed to be employed without

diet,—or rations, as is the colonial phrase. A cook will earn from £35 to £45 a year; laundresses from £30 to £40; other maid-servants from £20 to £30. The ordinary wages of a housemaid, who of course lives in the house, are 10s. a week. Men-servants, in the house, earn from £40 to £55 per annum.

There can I think be little doubt that the artisan with £3 a week, paying 4d. a pound for his meat and 7d. for a 4-lb. loaf, may live very plentifully. He probably pays about 1s. a week for the schooling of each of his children, but such is the comfort of his condition that he can do this without difficulty. I would not say to every artisan in London that he should save his money and pack up all that he has, and come out to Melbourne. Too often he cannot save any money. Frequently he is unfit to emigrate. It is, too generally, the case that the man who thus seeks new fortunes has to undergo some hardship before he can find his feet in the country of his adoption. I would not have any one believe that he can enter in upon the good things of the new world without trouble, without doubt, and without delay. Many a poor fellow burdened with wife and family, the best of whose strength has gone from him amidst the hardships of labour at home, has been tempted to go out, and when there has been unable to bear the roughness of beginning and has fallen in the struggle. But when the first struggle is over, and when the first battle has been won, the life of the artisan there is certainly a better life than he can find at home. He not only lives better, with more comfortable appurtenances around him, but he fills a higher position in reference to those around him, and has greater consideration paid to him, than would have fallen to his lot at home. He gets a better education for his children than he can in England, and may have a more assured hope of seeing them rise above himself, and has less cause to fear that they shall fall infinitely lower. Therefore I would say to any young man whose courage is high and whose intelligence is not below par, that he should not be satisfied to remain at home; but should come out,—to Melbourne, if that destination will in other respects suit him; and try to win a higher lot and a better fortune than the old country can afford to give him.

But if he take my advice and then turn recreant,—if he become idle or self-indulgent, or take to drink and vicious courses of pleasure,—then will woe betide him. For the fate of such a one in the colonies is worse even than it is at home.

CHAPTER IV.

BALLAARAT.

BALLARAT, the gold-field city,—or Ballaarat as the conscientious orthographists of the district insist on spelling it,—deserves a separate chapter to itself. Not that the two towns of that name,—Ballaarat and Ballaarat East,—with their vicinities comprise now—A.D. 1873—the most productive gold-fields of Australia, as they are beaten by those of Sandhurst; but that the place has been more noticeable than any other in the history of Australian gold, and more productive, taking its history back to the time when gold was first discovered there in 1851.

That was the great year of the discovery of Australian gold. I am not going into the deeply discussed question of the merits of this or that discoverer,—as to which jealousy is still rife both in New South Wales and Victoria. Taking the belief which I now find to be the most common in the colonies, I may say that Sir Roderick Murchison and Count Strzelecki both foretold the finding of Australian gold, basing their opinion on the geographical condition of the country; that Hargreaves, acting with others, first struck gold at Ophir in New South Wales; and that gold was first discovered, in Victoria, at Clunes, some few miles from the present city of Ballaarat. I will not venture to say who was the first discoverer, but a miner named Esmond was rewarded for the discovery. In New South Wales gold was declared to be found in April, 1851, and at Clunes in July, 1851, so that the interval between the two colonies was very small.

But, in regard to the discovery at Clunes, I think it is not to be doubted that gold was in fact found there eighteen months before it was declared. The date usually given as that of Esmond's discovery is July, 1851,—that being the very month in which the government of the new colony of Victoria commenced.

Both Hargreaves and Esmond had been gold-seekers in California, and were led to their discoveries by observation rather than by chance. There is, I believe, no doubt that gold had been found by chance previous to the discoveries of Hargreaves and Esmond,—but the finding of it had not led to great public results. Both Hargreaves and Esmond were rewarded.

Clunes is about 16 miles from Ballaarat, but the richness of the Ballaarat gold-fields soon followed the first discovery at Clunes. I am aware that I shall tread on very dangerous ground indeed if I assign either names or dates to the first movement of the soil at Golden Point, which is now built over by the present town,—Ballaarat East. But before the end of 1851 the rush to Ballaarat was an established thing, and whole streets of canvas tents were covering crowds of miners. We are told that men flocked to the place at the rate of 500 a day,—for whom no preparation had been made, no shelter built, no food brought together, no local laws enacted, no powers to enforce the laws existing. Its too great prosperity, its prospect of immediate and apparently unlimited wealth, was for a time more than the colony could bear. The minds of men were so disturbed that no man would remain at any old employment. Servants were out of the question. Shearers would not shear sheep unless they could earn their £6 or £7 a day. Gold commissioners with their clerks, police magistrates and policemen, were indispensable ; but who would be a clerk, or a policeman,—who even a magistrate or a commissioner,—when gold could be washed out of the dirt at the rate of ten ounces a day to each happy miner ? Food rose to incredible prices,—but then it was almost matter of indifference to a man whether he gave a shilling or a sovereign for his meal. The young government was almost beside itself,—and letters

full of frantic questions, eager fears, ambitious hopes, and
almost despair, must have reached our Colonial Office at
home by every mail. To whom did the gold belong? If
to the Crown, how should the Crown use and how protect
its rights? In what way might this new wealth be turned
to account, so that the colony at large might enjoy the prosperity? Might any man dig where he pleased,—and if so,
how should he be protected in his digging? What should
be his rights, and what his limits, and how should he be
made to pay for the now to him inestimable blessing of
protection?

It was at first decreed that a miner should pay a fee of
30*s.* a month for a licence to dig. This was very shortly
raised to £3 a month, though that amount was in truth
never collected. The idea of charging a miner £36 a year
for the privilege of digging arose from the desire to prevent
all the labour of the colony from throwing itself into the one
employment. But the outcry was so great that it was again
fixed at 30*s.* In October, 1854, the charge for a miner's
licence was £2 for three months. In the colony of Victoria the licence now costs 5*s.* a year. But the system of
licensing—of charging diggers even £18 per annum for the
privilege of mining—was not received with ready submission, and the money was collected with infinite difficulty.
Recusant diggers were hunted down by armed police; men
refused to pay; indignation meetings were held;—and at
length something like war broke out at Ballaarat. This was
in December, 1854,—when Sir Charles Hotham was governor, and about twelve months before his death. The diggers entrenched themselves on the gold-fields in a place that
was called the Eureka Stockade. Here they were attacked by
night, and thirty of them were killed. The ringleaders were
afterwards tried and acquitted,—and so the war was brought
to an end. But in those days there was certainly much
difficulty in governing the colony, and in bringing into
order a new state of things. It seemed for a time as though
the very wealth of the soil would prove the ruin of the
country.

Now it might be difficult to find a more quiet town than

Ballaarat, as it certainly would be to find one of the same age better built and more lavishly provided with all the appurtenances which municipalities require. It is certainly a most remarkable town. It struck me with more surprise than any other city in Australia. It is not only its youth, for Melbourne also is very young; nor is it the population of Ballaarat which amazes, for it does not exceed a quarter of that of Melbourne; but that a town so well built, so well ordered, endowed with present advantages so great in the way of schools, hospitals, libraries, hotels, public gardens, and the like, should have sprung up so quickly with no internal advantages of its own other than that of gold. The town is very pleasant to the sight, which is, perhaps, more than can be said for any other "provincial" town in the Australian colonies. When the year 1851 commenced, Ballaarat was an unknown name except perhaps here and there to a few shepherds. These words are written in the house of Messrs. Learmonth,—younger men than I, and therefore not old men to me,—who were the first pioneers in the country, and who ran the sheep which they brought with them from Van Diemen's Land over the hills adjacent to Ballaarat. They have given way to the gold-seekers, and, establishing themselves far enough from mines for rural serenity and pastoral comfort, are regarded as the territorial aristocrats of the district. Breathing their air and listening to their ideas, one feels as one does in the almost feudal establishment of some great English squire, who watches with a regret he cannot quite repress the daily encroachments made upon his life by the approaching hordes of some large neighbouring town.

Ballaarat has no navigable river. It is seventy or eighty miles from any possibility of sea-carriage. The land immediately around it is not fertile. It is high above the sea-level, and runs in gentle hills which twenty years since were thinly covered with gum-trees; and here wandered the flocks of a few patriarch pioneers. Then came first one or two rough seekers after gold, then half-a-dozen, then a score, then a rush,—and Ballaarat was established as one among the few great golden cities of the young world. I do not think

that there is any city equal to it that has sprung from gold
alone.

I myself believe in cities,—even though there should be
place in them for dishonest ambition, short-sighted policy,
and rowdiness. The dishonesty, the folly, and the rowdiness
are but the overboiling of the pot without which cannot be
had the hot water which is so necessary to our well-being. I
heard much abuse of Ballaarat from Ballaaratters. There
are three towns conjoined, Ballaarat, Ballaarat East, and
Sebastopol, with three town-halls, three municipalities, and
the like. The smaller towns will not consent to merge
themselves. There are in them men of obstruction, and
things cannot be done as they should be done. Money is
wasted; municipal funds are expended foolishly,—perhaps
fraudulently on an occasion. If this class would only see
with the eyes of that class, what a paradise it might be!
But they see with quite other eyes,—and what a pande-
monium it is becoming. So say the men of Ballaarat. Trade
is going to the dogs, because there is not sufficient protection;
—or else because a tariff of 20 per cent. on all imported
goods, levied in accordance with the wisdom of certain
ministers is destroying all trade by raising the price of bad
goods and driving serviceable goods out of the market. No
words which can here be used are strong enough to describe
the iniquity which some MacEvoy attributes to some
O'Brien, or some Murphy to some Jones or Smith. Population is falling off, so that shortly Ballaarat will be as a city
of the dead. Such are the accounts a stranger hears either
from this side or from that. One gentleman, who certainly
was very much in the dark as to the statistics of his town,
assured me that 20,000 people had gone out of Ballaarat in
two years. Another was angry with me because I hesitated
to believe that the place was ruined. I was assured that I
might hire 1,500 vacant houses at an hour's notice if I
wanted them. As for gold at Ballaarat, everybody knew
that that game had been played out!

Such were the records of some men. As far as the eye
went, I saw nothing but prosperity. Here I found that
most of the mines were worked by companies at wages paid

to the men,—and that a miner's wages averaged from 40*s.*
to 48*s.* a week,—the man working eight hours a day, and
thus reaching that acme of the workman's bliss—

> "Eight hours for work, and eight for play,
> Eight for sleep, and eight shillings a day."

And the necessaries of life, and the comforts, are at any rate
as cheap at Ballaarat as they are in England, in spite of
protective duties. Meat was about 2½*d.* a pound, and for
nothing did the workmen of Ballaarat pay more than his
brother in England, unless it be for clothes, for house-rent,
—and strong drinks, if he be that way given. Wages for all
work are high in proportion. In rural labour in the neighbourhood the farmer pays 20*s.* a week and rations, and at
harvest-time must pay double that amount. Female servants
in houses get 12*s.* a week,—or above £30 per annum.

Houses no doubt have been built too quickly,—as is
always found to be the case when some check comes to the
rising population of young towns. Such check had reached
Ballaarat when I was there,—the rush for the time being to
the gold-fields of Sandhurst ; and newly built houses were to
be seen empty. "There's a 'spec' that won't answer," said
a gentleman to me, pointing to a row of houses just finished,
but which from end to end showed no sign of habitation.
In two years' time some great quartz-crushing operation will
probably have been commenced ; and the then owner of the
row,—for the unfortunate first speculator will no doubt have
been sold out by his assignees,—will be making 30 per cent.
on his money.

There may be rowdiness, dishonesty and all other civic
sins in the manipulation of the municipal powers of Ballaarat
and other Australian cities ;—but as a rule the things which
a city requires are there. At Ballaarat this is conspicuously
the case. The hospital has more wards than it uses, and
more funds than it needs. As regards internal cleanliness
and sweetness, and external prettiness, it is perfect. The
Benevolent Institution,—which does the work that a poorhouse does with us,—gives either out-door relief or in-door
shelter and sustenance to all who cannot support themselves.

Such sustenance in Ballaarat—as indeed at all such institutions in Victoria—includes a thoroughly good dinner of meat and vegetables every day, with tea for breakfast and tea for "tea." It includes a bed perfectly clean, sitting-room, books, newspapers, comfortable clothes, and a garden to walk in infinitely superior to that enjoyed by many comfortable folk at home. Ballaarat has a public library, free to all the city,—and a mechanics' institute, with newspapers and privileges, at £1 a head. It has indeed every municipal luxury that can be named, including a public garden full of shrubs and flowers, and a lake of its own,—Lake Wendouree,—with a steamer and row-boats and regattas. It has a cricket-ground, and athletic games ; and it has omnibuses and cabs, which by their cleanliness and general excellence make a Londoner blush. For the privilege of seeing all these things with ease and comfort, and for much steady information, without exaggeration either on one side or the other, I have to thank that best of all mayors, Mr. R. Lewes, who reigned at Ballaarat at the time of my visit.

But as yet I have said nothing of the gold-mines which have made Ballaarat what it is. Among Victorian gold-fields it is famous for alluvial dirt to be washed,—not for quartz to be crushed, as is the case with its rival town of Sandhurst, of which I shall speak in the next chapter. But the reader must not therefore suppose that Ballaarat is a place of mere surface scratching, an agglomeration of gullies from which the mud is shovelled into cradles, a congregation of "fossickers"—men who search about, picking and washing a bit of earth here and a bit there, or upper-air miners who know nothing of large operations. The alluvial dirt which produces the greater portion of the wealth of Ballaarat has not only to be brought up many hundred feet from under the surface, but it has to be sought for through underground passages thousands of feet in length, and has to be followed up by geological deductions which too often fail in their promises.

I went down one such mine called " Winter's Freehold," descending 450 feet in an iron cage. I was then taken 4,000 feet along an underground tramway in a truck drawn

E

by a horse. At the end of that journey I was called upon
to mount a perpendicular ladder about 20 feet high, and
was then led along another tramway running apparently at
right angles to the first. From this opened out the cross
passages in which the miners were at work. Here we saw
the loose alluvial grit, so loose that a penknife would remove
it, lying on the solid rock,—on it and under it,—to the
breadth I was told of some four feet; for though I saw
the bottom of the grit, where it lay on its bed, I could
not see the top where it was covered. Here and there
among the grit, with candle held up, and some experienced
miner directing my eye, I could see the minute specs of
gold, in search of which these vast subterranean tunnels had
been made. It seemed to be but a speck here and there,
—so inconsiderable as to be altogether unworth the search.
But the mining men who were with us, the manager, deputy-
manager, or shareholders,—for on such occasions one
hardly knows who are the friends who accompany one,—
expressed themselves highly satisfied.

I was told that £150,000 had been expended on this
single mine up to the present time, and that the machinery
was the finest in the colony. Perhaps the finest machinery
in the colony may be seen at more than one mine in the
colony. But I was informed that hitherto the results had
not been magnificent. There was, however, a good time
coming, and all the money expended would certainly come
back with copious interest. I hope that it may be so. We
were two hours in seeing the mine,—and I must say that as
regards immediate enjoyment the two hours were not well
spent. The place was wet and dirty and dark, the progress
was tedious, and the result to the eye very poor. But such
is the result to all amateur inspectors of mines. When we
had extricated ourselves from the bowels of the earth we
ascended to a platform on the top of the machinery, to
which the wash-dirt is carried that it may there be puddled
and the gold extracted. The height enables the water and
mud to run off. The dirt is placed in a round flat recep-
tacle or trough, into which water runs, and an instrument
somewhat like a harrow is worked through it. The water and

mud are amalgamated, and the height enables them to run off together. The gold by its own weight falls to the bottom mixed with stones or shingle. This is afterwards sent down to an open spout below, through which water runs, a man the while working it with a fork prepared for the purpose. Again the stones and mud pass off with the water, and again the gold remains behind, sinking to the bottom by its own weight. When all has escaped that will escape, and the stones that will not fall have been thrown out, then the specks of gold are seen lying thick, collected in the little furrows which are marked on the bottom of the spout. To the uninitiated eye the product of all this costly labour still seems to be small.

After all this the gold is smelted into bars and sold to the merchants or bankers. We went to the offices of another company,—the Band of Hope and Albion Consols, —to see the smelting. In this operation there is nothing wonderful. The small gold—for it is all small in comparison with the nuggets of which we have heard so much and which are now very rare in Australia—is poured into an earthen pot, is melted, is poured out into moulds, is then washed so that it may have a clean face, and is straightway sent to the bank. At present the greater part of the gold found at Ballaarat when thus prepared is worth something over £4 an ounce. At this Band of Hope mine they raise about 3,000 ounces of gold a month, at an expense of about half its value. The other half is divided among the shareholders, and gives an average interest of £12 15s. per cent. on the capital expended on the work. This, in a business subject to great risk, with bank interest at 8 and 9 per cent., does not seem to be a very rich result.

We also saw a quartz-crushing machine at work,—for quartz is raised at Ballaarat, though in much less quantity than the wash-dirt. The nature of a quartz-crusher I have described in speaking of Gympie, the great Queensland gold-field. In Victoria, as I have said, Sandhurst is the great quartz district ;—but there are sanguine people who predict a vast wealth of quartz reefs at Ballaarat after the wash-dirt has been all extracted.

CHAPTER V.

HAVING thus described Ballaarat, which in point of architectural excellence and general civilised city comfort is at
present certainly the metropolis of the Australian gold-
fields, I should lay myself open to charges of gross partiality
if I omitted to give some account of Sandhurst,—which
intends to surpass Ballaarat, and to become mightier and
more world-famous than that very mighty and world-famous
place. I do not pretend to say what may be the result of
the race.

My readers have, no doubt, heard of the Bendigo gold-
fields. I think it by no means improbable that some of
them,—in England,—may never have heard the name of
Sandhurst as connected with gold. I had not done so
when I first landed in Australia, though I had been often
told of Bendigo, having some hazy idea that the place had
called itself after a prize-fighter, and therefore must be a
very rowdy place indeed. I imagine that some such feeling
must have been predominant with the people of the place
when Bendigo, as a name, was dropped, and Sandhurst,—
which is not only euphonious, but which carries with it also
a certain mixed idea of youthful energy and military discipline,—was chosen in its stead. Sandhurst means to go
ahead, and become a great city. In regard to the production of gold it has gone very much ahead. As a city, when
I was there, it was neither handsome nor commodious. It
had the appearance, which is common to all new mining
towns, of having been scratched up violently out of the

body of the earth by the rake of some great infernal deity, who had left everything behind him dirty, uncouth, barren, and disorderly! Any one who has seen the mining towns as they rose in Cornwall and Glamorganshire must have observed the same ugliness. At Sandhurst you see heaps of upturned dry soil here and there, dislocated whims, rows of humble houses built just as they were wanted, shops with gewgaw fronts put up at a moment's notice, drinking-bars in abundance, here and there an attempt at architecture, made almost invariably by some banking company eager to push itself into large operations;—but with it all a look of eager, keen energy which would redeem to the mind the hideous objects which meet the eye, were it not that the mind becomes conscious of the too-speculative nature of the work done,—of the gambling propensities of the people around,—and is driven to feel that the buying and selling of mining shares cannot be done by yea, yea, and nay, nay.

In Melbourne there is the "verandah;"—in Sandhurst there is a "verandah;" in Ballaarat there is a "verandah." The verandah is a kind of open exchange,—some place on the street pavement apparently selected by chance, on which the dealers in mining shares do congregate. What they do, or how they carry on their business when there, I am unable to explain. But to the stranger, or the passer by, they do not look lovely. He almost trembles lest his eyes should be picked out of his head as he goes. He has no business there, and soon learns to walk on the other side of the road. And he hears strange tales which make him feel that the innocence of the dove would not befriend him at all were he to attempt to trade in those parts. I think there is a racing phrase as to "getting a tip." The happy man who gets a tip learns something special as to the competence or incompetence of a horse. There are a great many tips in gold mines which fall into the fortunate hands of those who attend most closely, and perhaps with most unscrupulous fidelity, to the business of the verandahs. The knowing ones know that a certain claim is going to give gold. The man who has the tip sells out at a low price,—sells out a certain number of shares, probably to a friend who holds the tip with him. The price is quoted on the share list, and the unfortunate non-tipped sell out also, and the fortunate tipped one buys up all. A claim is not going to give gold,—and the reverse happens. Or a claim is salted;—gold is surreptitiously introduced, is then taken out, and made the base of a fictitious prosperity. The tipped ones sell, and the untipped buy. It is easy to see that the game is very pretty; but then it is dangerous. It has certainly become very popular. One is told at Melbourne that all are playing at it,—clergymen, judges, ladies, old ladies and young, married ladies and single,—old men and boys, fathers unknown to their sons, and sons unknown to their fathers, mothers unknown to their daughters, daughters unknown to their mothers,—masters and servants, tradesmen and their apprentices. "You shall go from one end of Collins Street to another," a man said to me, "and you will hardly meet one who has not owned a share or a part of a share." Gold-mining in Victoria is as was to us the railway mania some twenty-four years ago. Melbourne no doubt is the centre of the trade in shares, but low beneath the surface in the mines of Sandhurst lie the hearts of the gold-gamblers.

At Ballaarat the chief produce of gold is still obtained from alluvial dirt,—from dirt which is indeed extracted by deep working out of the bowels of the earth, and not, as at first, from the channels of rivers and the crevices of mountain gullies,—but still from alluvial dirt, which, when extracted, is washed. The gold remains after the washing and then the operation is at an end. At Sandhurst the gold is got by quartz-crushing. The gold-bearing rock is brought up in great masses,—thousands and thousands of tons of stone, which is called quartz. This is crushed by huge machinery, and the gold is separated from the dirt by the use of quick-silver and water. The washing of alluvial soil is the readier way of getting gold, but the quartz-crushing is the more important. Of the alluvial dirt there must, or at any rate there may, soon be an end. The geologists say that the crushers of quartz may eat up whole mountains, and still go on finding stone that will give gold. Looking at a table now before me as to quartz crushed at Sandhurst in 1871, I find that 2 oz. 14 dwt. to the ton of quartz was the highest amount extracted, and that 4 dwt. to the ton is the lowest quantity there quoted. The proportion that will pay depends of course on the amount of outlay. Some of the gold-bearing stone is brought up 800 feet, and some only 100. In some mines the levels and cross-cuts and underground passages are worked for long distances, perhaps for a mile, without gold. In others the gold is struck at once. It is impossible, therefore, to say what proportion will pay; but it is certain that in many mines half an ounce, or two sovereigns, to a ton of rock will pay well. It is on record that 250 oz. of gold were extracted on the Bendigo gold-fields from one ton of stone,—fifteen years ago. But the great glory of Sandhurst was reached, when an average of 9 oz. per ton was extracted from 264 tons of quartz, taken from " The Great Extended Hustler's mine."

I venture to extract a quotation from a published " Digest of the Dividend-Paying Companies of the Bendigo Gold-Fields," which is now before me,—given in the shape of a note,—because it purports to be a record of the greatest event of the year 1871.

" NOTE.—On October 18th, the greatest event of the year's quartz-mining occurred. For some days previously the gathering of the Extended Hustler's Tribute amalgam created much interest in mining circles; 6,400 oz. aggregate of amalgam was reached when the company proceeded to retort, and betting, except with those intimately acquainted with the nature of the stone, was in favour of over 3,000 oz. of gold. A little after 7 p.m. of the 18th the Oriental Bank solved all doubts by exhibiting the Tribute Company's cake of 2,564 oz., and shortly afterwards the Great Extended Hustler's Tribute declared the largest dividend ever paid on Sandhurst,—6s. 6d. per share, equal to £9,100. The yield was obtained from 264 tons, reef 18 feet thick, average 9 oz. per ton."

I saw this interesting cake at the Oriental Bank in Mel-bourne, on which occasion the manager kindly offered to give it to me on condition that I should carry it away.

All prosperous trades have a slang of their own,—certain terms used to keep outsiders at a distance, and to create that feeling of esoteric privilege which we all like to have in regard to matters which we think we understand. A man who only uses horses can never talk in professional language to a man who breeds them and deals in them and lives with them. A layman in politics, let him be ever so anxious for his country, is all abroad when conversing with a member of parliament about bills and acts, about notices of motion and "the previous question." It is very much so with mining. Everything is told to the visiting stranger, but I don't think he is intended to understand anything. What with tributes and claims, with leads and lodes, with shafts and levels and cross-cuts and veins, with reefs and gullies, with quartz, amalgam, tailings, and mullock,—I am by no means sure of the spelling of that last word,—he is made to feel that he is an outsider, and that he cannot learn mining in a day. At Sandhurst I felt this very strongly;—and my reader will probably feel as I did. He will simply acknowledge to himself the fact that a cake of gold containing 2,564 oz.,—and worth about £10,000,—is a very large cake indeed.

The names selected by various companies at the Sandhurst gold-fields deserve attention. Sandhurst, which now aspires to be the leading Australian gold-field, and which certainly turns out more gold than any other, boasts at present no less than 1,200 different companies. I should say that there were 1,200 in the early part of 1872. The number will probably be very greatly increased before these words are published. The names chosen for these companies are certainly very quaint. There are not less than fourteen " New Chum " Companies, and there are three or four " Old Chum " Companies. There are the Peg Leg, the Perfect Cure, the Who can Tell, the Great Extended Who can Tell, the Sons of Freedom, the Sir Walter Scott, the Sailor Prince, the Royal Louisa, the Lord Byron, the Little Chum, the Jonadab, the Hand and Band, the Happy Day, the Happy-go-Lucky, the Great Extended South Golden Pyke, the Go by Gold, the Charles Gavan Duffy, the Gladstone,—indeed there are five or six Gladstone Companies;—and, to be fair, I must add that there is a Disraeli Company; I do not, however, find it quoted among those that are paying dividends. But, among all names at Sandhurst, the greatest name, the most thriving, the best known, and the name in highest repute, is—" Hustler." Whence came the appellation I do not distinctly know, but I believe that there once was—perhaps still is—a happy Hustler. If so, even the Marquis of Granby among publicans has not been a more prolific godfather than has Mr. Hustler among Sandhurst miners. What with original Hustler Companies and Tribute Hustler Companies, with simple Hustlers, and Extended Hustlers, and Great Extended Hustlers, with North Hustlers, and South Hustlers, and with Extended North and South Hustlers, the companies who claim the happy name are difficult to count. There are at any rate two dozen of them, and all, or nearly all, are doing well.

Of these 1,200 different companies, about one-third are, so called, Tribute Companies. The parent company—for instance the parent Great Extended Hustlers—lets off a piece of land, or a claim, to a set of men, generally working miners, having performed a certain portion of the preliminary work,—having opened the shaft and put up machinery, and probably shown that gold is to be had for the labour. The claim is let on a certain tribute,—the tributers or sub-company agreeing to pay a fixed proportion of the gold extracted to the original company The miners are very fond of going into this kind of speculation, as it opens up to them the chance of making a fortune. But on the other hand it opens up to them also the chance—and very often the reality—of working for nothing. The expenses of the mine and the tribute which is exacted will not unfrequently consume all the gold produced ; or,—worse than that,—the expense of the mine will go on, and there will be no produce. The tributer will not only be working for nothing, but will also be called on to pay towards the continuance of the enterprise. He must live the while,—and would thus seem to be debarred from such speculation unless he be possessed of capital. But in fact such is not the case. A miner at Sandhurst, when I was there, could earn from £2 10s. to £3 a week, and could live well on 20s. Two men, or more, would form a partnership, of which the one half would work for wages, and the other half on a tribute claim. The wages would suffice to support the whole, and even to pay up a certain amount of " calls." Should the speculation turn out well, the profits would be divided among the lot. The speculation often does turn out well, and men become suddenly enriched. It often turns out badly,—and in such cases the miners have worked barely for a subsistence. At such places as Sandhurst it is said that in this way a grand spirit of commercial enterprise is created and fostered. Men without capital are enabled to enter in upon the joys of commercial speculation. There is, however, another way of looking at it ; and many no doubt will think that the commercial speculation is simple gambling on a great scale. I have no doubt myself that the miners who work simply for wages are in the long run more prosperous than they who work on tribute. A man's wages represent to him with clear and well-defined reality the very sweat of his brow. If there be enough for him to save something, and if he be given to saving, he will save the surplus of money so earned. But that which comes to him in a lump, from some happy chance, from some pocket of gold found in the bowels of the earth, from some rich crushing of quartz with which it has been his lot to become connected, exalts him suddenly, upsets his head,—and is apt to disappear as rapidly as it came. All this of course is old-world teaching and grandmother's tales. I feel as I write it that it is too trite to be written. But I feel at the same time that it is impossible to write of gold-mining in Australia without repeating the old lesson. No doubt instances may be adduced of men who have made and have kept splendid fortunes by gold-mining,—of men who have done so without capital, by small speculations at first, and by extended operations as the means have come to them. I have heard of men so blessed,—and could name one or two. But I have heard of no case in which the man so blessed was represented to me as living after a blessed fashion. I have, however, heard of cases by the score in which the questionable blessing has never been achieved,—as to which I have been told, frequently by the speculators themselves, that had they stopped here or had they stopped there, they would have made two, four, six, ten, or twenty thousand pounds as the case may have been. There has been a shake of the head, and a soft regret; and I always felt that I liked the man the better in that he had lost it all, than I should have done had he become per- manently successful.

As regards the working miners, including all those who manage the works and overlook the machinery, I am bound to say that they are a fine body of able and industrious men. This is so on all the large gold-fields, and nowhere more noticeably than at Sandhurst. They are intelligent, manly, and independent,—altogether free from that subservience which the domination of capital too often produces in most fields of labour. I have spoken, perhaps as strongly as I know how to speak, of the gambling propensities of the population of a gold-mining town. I should be wrong if I did not speak as strongly of the efforts which are made by such communities,—which in Australia are always made when the communities become large and apparently fixed,— to ameliorate the condition of the people. The hospitals are excellent, the provision for the indigent is so good as almost to promote indigence, the schools are well conducted and well filled, the churches are sufficient, and the clergy- men are supported. The money comes freely and is freely expended. And in no community are the manners of the people more courteous or their conduct more decent. Of course there is drinking. The idle men drink,—would-be gentlemen, who are trying to speculate, without apparent means of livelihood, drink,—miners who are not mining, having what they call a spell, or holiday, will drink. But the working miner is a sober man, with a sober family; and of such the bulk of the mining population is made up. In England working men drink;—work by day, and drink by night; then half work by day and double drink by night,— till the thing comes soon to an end. In Australia, as a rule, the working man does not drink while he works. The shearer does not drink; the shepherd and boundary- rider do not drink; the reaper and ploughman do not drink;—nor does the miner drink, Let them be idle for a while; let them take their wages and go away for a "spell;" —then they will drink as no Englishman ever drinks, drink down in a fortnight the earnings of a year. But there is less of this with miners than with shearers or ploughmen. The miner gambles,—and is so saved from the worse vice of drinking.

And the gambling of the miner has about it a certain redeeming manliness which is altogether wanting to the denizen of the race-course or of the roulette-table. Though he gambles, he works and produces. The gambling is but an excrescence on his genuine industry. The Sandhurst regular miner works in shifts, of eight hours each shift, throughout the day and night. The gold is being sought and found, dug out and dragged up, and crushed out of its matrix, the quartz, for four-and-twenty hours a day, during six days of the week. And the skilled miner, by eight hours' work a day, may earn at least 9s. a day in a country in which he and his wife and children may live comfortably —and as regards food with absolute plenty—for 4s. a day. The gold-miner at Sandhurst who keeps himself simply to his work, and takes no part in New Extended Great Chum Tributes, has, as work goes on in the world, by no means an unhappy lot.

I went down the shaft of one mine,—the Great Extended Hustler, I think it was called,—600 feet below the surface, and was received with the greatest courtesy. I am bound to say that I saw nothing that was worth seeing, and that I understood nothing of all that was told to me. This is an almost disgraceful declaration to make, after one has pretended to understand all that was said. But it was so with me, and is so I take it with all travellers. The experienced and good-natured professional miners who conduct the strangers are anxious that everything should be made plain. To them everything is plain. But the very A B C of their necessary knowledge is probably Hebrew to the listener, who is too grateful for the attention paid to him to tell the kind teacher how utterly unintelligible to him is the whole matter in question. It was so with me;—but this I saw, and could have seen as well above the earth as by going below,—that tons of grey stone were dragged up, that the grey stone was all stamped and crushed into powder by machinery, and that out of the powder gold was got in certain proportions, —so many ounces, or more probably so many pennyweights, to the ton of stone,—and that, as the result was good or bad, dividends were divided or were not divided among the speculators.

CHAPTER VI.

I WENT by coach from Melbourne to Gippsland with a friend, partly with a view of visiting that district generally, and partly that I might see the eastern gold-fields of the colony. I had indeed become very tired of gold,—which to a traveller who enjoys none of the excitement arising from the hope of acquiring it, is but a wearisome object. I did not desire to go down more mines, and yet I felt that I should not be strong-minded enough to save myself from further descents. I think I should have taken the Gippsland gold-fields on credit, had I not been told that the scenery around them was peculiarly beautiful. I was specially desired not to miss Woods Point,—which indeed is not in Gippsland, but which could be visited from Gippsland by any one who would trust himself among the mountains on horseback. From Woods Point I could return to Melbourne by a direct road, so as to avoid the disagreeable task of retracing my steps over the same path. As far as scenery was concerned, I was certainly repaid for the labour of a somewhat laborious journey. Gippsland is the south-eastern district of Victoria. It has I believe lately been divided into counties,—or rather, a portion of it has been so far civilised. It is separated from the Murray district of Victoria by spurs of the so-called Australian Alps, among which lie the eastern gold-fields.

We started by one of Cobb's coaches at one o'clock in the day, and reached the little town of Rosedale in Gippsland at ten the next morning. Cobb's coaches have the

name of being very rough,—and more than once I have
been warned against travelling by them. They were not
fit, I was told, for an effeminate Englishman of my time of
life. The idea that Englishmen,—that is, new-chums, or
Englishmen just come from home,—are made of paste,
whereas the Australian native or thoroughly acclimatized, is
steel all through, I found to be universal. On hearing such
an opinion as to his own person, a man is bound to sacrifice
himself, and to act contrary to the advice given, even though
he perish in doing so. This journey I made and did not perish
at all ;—and on arriving at Rosedale had made up my mind
that twenty hours on a Cobb's coach through the bush in
Australia does not inflict so severe a martyrdom as did in
the old days a journey of equal duration on one of the time-
famous, much-regretted old English mails. More space is
allowed you for stretching your legs on the seat, and more
time for stretching your legs at the stages. The road of
course is rough,—generally altogether unmade,—but the
roughness lends an interest to the occasion, and when the
coach is stuck in a swamp,—as happens daily,—it is pleasant
to remember that the horses do finally succeed, every day,
in pulling it out again. On this road there is a place called
the Glue Pot, extending perhaps for a furlong, as to which
the gratified traveller feels that now, at any rate, the real
perils of travel have been attained. But the horses, rolling
up to their bellies in the mud, do pull the coach through.
This happens in the darkness of night, in the thick forest,—
and the English traveller in his enthusiasm tells the coachman that no English whip would have looked at such a
place even by daylight. The man is gratified, lights his
pipe, and rushes headlong into the next gully.

The land between Melbourne and Gippsland, through
the county of Mornington, is very poor ; as it is also for
some distance in Gippsland itself. Then the timber becomes less thick and the grasses rich. When first taken up
the country was used for sheep ;—but it was not found to be
good for wool, and the sheep have now given place to
cattle. A large proportion of the beef with which Melbourne is fed is fattened on the Gippsland runs. Here,

as throughout Victoria, all the best of the soil has been
already purchased, and is for the most part in the hand of
large owners—of men whose successors will be lords of vast
territorial properties, and not of small free-selecters or farmers.
Throughout the colony it is impossible not to see how futile
have been the efforts of legislation to prevent the accumulation of large domains in the hands of successful men. It
has been thought by one ministry after another to be wise,
—or, at any rate, to be expedient,—to break up the hold-
ings of the great squatters, so that there should be no territorial magnates. The law has done all that it could be
made to do, compatibly with justice,—sometimes perhaps
more than it could do with that condition,—to make the
colony a paradise for small landowners, and a purgatory for
wealthy men who should attempt to accumulate acres.
Politicians ambitious of being statesmen, who can reach
power only by the aid of universal suffrage, are prone to
look for popularity, and popularity in Victoria has much
depended on adherence to the interests of the free-selecter.
As I have said elsewhere, the interests of the small buyer
of land are entitled to warmer sympathy than those of the
would-be territorial magnates. One still dreams of a happy
land in which every man with his wife and children shall
live happily and honestly on his own acres,—owing neither
rent nor submission to any lord. It may be that this feeling has been stronger with Victorian politicians than the
love of political power. It is at any rate the feeling by
which they claim to have been actuated, and they have
worked hard to carry out their theory. But the wages of
commerce and the enterprise of the intelligent have been
stronger than any bonds which statesmen or legislators
could forge. Wealth has been accumulated by a few, and
wealth has procured the land in spite of the laws. Though
cabinet ministers and land commissioners have had the
land in their hands to sell under such laws as they have
pleased to pass, though they have had a power entrusted
to them as managers and agents greater than any confided
by us to our ministers at home, though it has been declared
by politicians that there should be no land magnates in

Victoria, the rich have bought the land; and now vast territories are possessed by individuals which more than rival in area—and in course of time will rival in value—the possessions of great families at home. This is hardly so in the United States,—is not so certainly to the same extent. There men seek to build up wealth in the cities rather than in the country, and prefer shares and scrip and commercial speculation to land. Why there should be this difference in the same race, when settled away from home in different regions, some one some day no doubt will tell us.

To fatten cattle is the present business of the Gippsland squire. Cattle, no doubt, are bred there, but it seemed to be more usual to buy them young from some other district, and have them driven up over long distances to the Gippsland pastures. I do not pride myself on having a good eye for a bullock,—but those I saw seemed to be very big and very fat, very tame and very stupid. Why a bullock who has a paddock of seven or eight thousand acres in which to roam should make so little of himself as these beasts do in Australia I cannot understand. At home I think they are more troublesome and have higher hearts. I went out one morning at four A.M. to see a lot drafted out of a herd for sale. "Cutting out" is the proper name for this operation. Two or three men on horseback, of whom I considered myself to be by far the most active, drove some hundreds of them into a selected corner of the paddock called a "camp." There was no enclosure, no hurdles, no gates, no flogging, very little hallooing, and very little work. This camp happened to be in a corner; but camps for cattle generally are in the centre of the field, a bare spot,—made bare by its repeated use for this purpose,—to which the bullocks go when they are told, and on which they stand quietly till the operation of cutting out is over. On the occasion on which I was assisting, the owner himself was the "cutter out." He rode in among the herd, and selecting with his eye some animal sufficiently obese for market purposes, signified to the doomed one that he should leave the herd. There was a stock-rider to assist him, and the stock-rider also signified

F

his intention.   It seemed to be done altogether by the eye.
The beast went out and stood apart, till he was joined by a
second selected one and then by a third.   On this occasion
some thirty or forty were selected,—either as many as were
fit or as the owner desired to sell.   These were at once
driven off on the way to Melbourne, and the others were
allowed to go back to their grazing.   I had looked for
racing, and cracking of stock-whips, and horses falling, and
some wild work among the forest trees.   I would not know-
ingly have left my bed at four o'clock to see so tame a performance.   At least for half its distance the road up to
Melbourne is not fenced off from the timber, and consists
of devious forest tracts; but these tame brutes never make
their way out into the woods on the journey, as they
might do.

My friend and I bought two horses and two saddles, and
started from Rosedale on our journey to the mines.   We
had met some influential gentlemen of the district—a judge,
a resident magistrate, and an inspector of police—who
were united in their assurance that if we went without
a guide we should certainly be lost in the bush.   Now my
friend was a man of mark, whose loss would have been
severely felt by the colony, and for his security we were
furnished with a mounted trooper, or policeman, to show us
our way, and generally take care of us on our expedition.
We certainly needed him, and, as I believe, would have
been sleeping now in some Gippsland gully but for his
assistance.   Our first day's march was to Walhalla, a mining
town of great wealth to which there is literally no road.
Our journey was one of about forty miles;—for the latter
half of it, continuously through forests, and as continuously
up and down mountains.   These were so steep that it was
often impossible to sit on horseback.   As the weather was
very hot our toil was great, and I shall never forget the
welcome with which I greeted the beer-shop on the Thompson River.   The scenery through these mountains is magnificent,—when it can be seen.   But such is the continuity
and contiguity of the trees, that it becomes impossible for
miles together to see either the hill-tops or the depths of

the valleys. Going down to the Thompson River, and again down into Walhalla, we found it to be impossible to ride ; and yet we knew that immense masses of machinery had been taken down by bullocks for the use of the miners. We were told that very many bullocks had been destroyed at the work. I could not have believed that there had been such a traffic across the mountains and through the forests, had I not afterwards seen the things at Walhalla.

At last we got to the place, very tired and very footsore, and had bedrooms allocated to us in the hotel close to the quartz-crushing machine, which goes on day and night eating up the rock which is dragged forth from the bowels of the earth. The noisy monster continued his voracious meal without cessation for a moment, so that sleep was out of the question. To the residents of the inn the effect was simply somniferous. Their complaint was that from twelve o'clock on Saturday night when the monster begins to keep his Sabbath, to twelve o'clock on Sunday night when his religious observances are over, the air is so burdened by silence that they can neither talk by day nor sleep by night.

The mining town which has been dignified by the name of Walhalla lies at the bottom of a gully from which the wooded sides rise steeply. Through it meanders a stream which is now, of course, contaminated by the diggings and pumpings, and gold-washing and quartz-crushing, which have befallen the locality. Nevertheless it has a peculiar beauty of its own, and a picturesque interest arising in part from the wooded hills which so closely overhang it,—but partly also from the quaintness of a town so placed. The buildings, consisting of banks, churches, schools, hotels, managers' houses, and miners' cottages, lie along the stream, or are perched up on low altitudes among the trees. There is something like a winding street through it, which is nearly a mile long,—though indeed it is difficult sometimes to distinguish between the river and the street ; but there is no road to it from any place in the world ;—and even the tracks by which it is to be left are not easy of discovery. We went down to it by the "Little Joe," the Little Joe being a hill-side, and I hope I may never have to go down the Little Joe again with a tired horse behind me. We left it by a path as steep and so hidden that we should never have found it without a guide. As it was, the mayor conducted us out of Walhalla with some solemnity.

And yet in this singular place there are, or seem to be, congregated all the necessaries and most of the luxuries of life. There was a pianoforte in the hotel sitting-room, and framed pictures hanging on the wall,—just as there might be in Birmingham. And there was a billiard-table,—at which unwashed earth-soiled diggers were playing, and playing, too, very well. At what cost must the pianoforte and the billiard-table have been brought down the mountain track! Nevertheless the charge for billiards was no more than sixpence a game; and no charge whatever was made for the piano!

The great mine at Walhalla when I was there was the Long Tunnel. Shares in the Long Tunnel were hardly to be had for money; but, bought even at most exaggerated prices, gave almost endless interest. I went down the Long Tunnel,—and came up again. As usual I found below a dirty grubbing world. Men were earning between £2 and £3 a week, living hardly,—though always plenteously; and speculating in gold with their savings. But here, as elsewhere, they were courteous and kind. Their children are all educated, and if churches and meeting-houses may be taken as a proof of religion they are religious. I was told that the place contained about 1,500 inhabitants. I cannot repeat too often that I have never met more courteous men than the gold-miners of Australia.

We stayed but one night, and then proceeded on our journey, still taking our mounted guide, and for the first ten miles were under the special guardianship of the mayor,— who was to be looked upon, I was told, as a deputation from the town in honour of my friend. A very pleasant fellow we found the Mayor of Walhalla, and we parted from him in great kindness, even though he did lose the way in the forest, and take us, all for nothing, up and down one mountain side. When he parted from us our trusty trooper was a safer guide. This man was, I believe, no more than an ordinary policeman. The rural policemen of the colonies, who have to pass over wide districts, are all mounted. But they carry themselves higher, and stand much higher among their fellow citizens, than do the men of the same class with us. We are apt to separate men into two classes, —and define each man by saying that he is or that he is not a gentleman. This man was a private policeman. Had I not known the fact, I should have taken him for a gentleman. Even as it is I rather think that I regard him in that light. He was a fine, powerful fellow, well mannered, able to talk on all subjects, extremely courteous,—and he amused us greatly by explaining to us why it was that a policeman must be always more than a match for at any rate two rogues. He was an Irishman,—of course. In the colonies those who make money are generally Scotchmen, and those who do not are mostly Irishmen. He had probably come out because his family could do nothing for him at home. I hope that he may live to be General-in-Chief of the Victorian police. He took us through the mountains to an old and apparently worn-out diggings called Edwards' Reef,—a miserable, melancholy place, surrounded by interminable forests, in which unhappy diggers had sunk holes here and there, so that one wondered that the children did not all perish by falling into them. But even at Edwards' Reef there was an hotel, though I was at a loss to imagine by whom it could be supported. It was a large wooden building, now nearly falling to the ground; though doubtless it had once been alive with the sound of miners' voices in the days when there was gold in these quarters.

From Edwards' Reef we went on to Woods Point, having changed our policeman. It seems that the magistrates had ordered that we should be taken in safety as far as the latter place. We passed another day in traversing endless forests, and in ascending and descending ravines. Here and there, in the densest parts of the forests, we came on the old tracks of miners, finding the holes which they had dug in search of gold. How many a heart must have been broken,—how many a back nearly broken, among these mountains! The ascents and descents here were very steep, and on one occasion we submitted to be pulled up, hanging on to our horses' tails,—an operation which I had not seen since I hunted, many years ago, in Carmarthenshire. On this journey we had an adventure. At an inn among the mountains,—for here and there one comes upon an inn, though there are no roads,—we found two girls who were desirous of going to a wedding which was to be held in a neighbouring gully. Luckily, or perhaps unluckily, the mounted mailman came up, driving two spare horses before him. So the girls at once borrowed the horses, and the inn afforded one side-saddle. The girl who mounted without the side-saddle rode well, and might have reached the wedding triumphantly; but the other was somewhat at fault, even with the side-saddle. She was bold enough, but had probably never been on horseback before. We had gone on during the trouble of the saddle as there appeared to be some bashfulness in completing the arrangement; but before long the poor maiden's steed was after us. He had run away with her, and for a moment or two I thought she must have perished among the trees,—but as the beast passed us he shied, and deposited his burden close at the feet of the horse I was riding. She was shaken, for awhile speechless, soiled, and wretched; but before long she proclaimed her intention of walking to the wedding. The distance was not above six miles through the woods. The other girl like a true friend dismounted, that she might walk with her companion, and the mailman with his spare horses proceeded on with us to Jericho.

Jericho was another digging town, down in a gully, at which men were grubbing for gold, scooping out great holes in and near the bed of the river. The great forests rose steep on each side, and the place was grandly picturesque. We were told that Jericho not long since had been a prosperous place for gold-seekers. Thence we ascended a hill to Matlock, another gold-digging town, very high up, very bleak, and the most wretched place I ever saw. Some one there declared that Matlock was the highest inhabited spot in Victoria. This was in February, a summer month;— but even then the cold was intense. There is no gold now at Matlock, and I could not understand what induced the few unfortunate inhabitants to remain there. Though it is a difficult thing to establish a town or village, it is still more difficult to disestablish it. But Matlock will soon disestablish itself under the effect of the winds of heaven. From Matlock we descended four miles into Woods Point.

Woods Point is a gold-field of great importance,—of very great importance indeed in the estimation of the Woods-Pointers. It has been very rich, and is still producing gold in remunerating quantities. But I met nowhere gold-seekers so wedded to gold as were the heroes of Woods Point. I was allowed the privilege of dining with some of the great men of the place, and I thought that I should hardly have been permitted to leave the room alive, because I expressed an opinion that wool was of more importance to the colonies generally than the precious metal, which I found to be so well loved at this place. Oh, men of Woods Point, if ever these words should meet your ears, know how utterly unconvinced I was by your oratory, though in arguments I was unable to stand up against the fervour of your eloquence! At Woods Point I inspected a mine, but contented myself with inspecting it from the surface. Every opportunity, however, was given me to go below, had I chosen to avail myself of the courtesy of my conductors.

Woods Point, like Walhalla, is a gully or ravine,—though less singular than Walhalla, because there is a coach-road running through it. The scenery around it is very lovely, —so much so as to inspire a feeling of sorrow that so much beauty should be desecrated by miners. Altogether the beauty of the country through which we had passed, and through which we did pass on our way back to Melbourne, contradicted the too general assertion that Australia is destitute of lovely scenery.

Three days more, with a pleasant rest at a friend's house on the road,—as to which I have spoken in another chapter, referring to the Yering wine,—brought us back to Melbourne. On the way down we passed through a country now well known for its enormous trees,—all gum-trees of various sorts, or Eucalypti as they are called by the learned.

At the land office in Melbourne I heard tidings of one enormous tree which had lately been discovered in this region, prostrate over a river-bed, and of which the remaining portion,—for the head had been broken off in the fall, —measured 435 ft. in length. The gentleman by whom this monster was found had been sent out by the commissioners of lands to inspect the timber in the ranges of the watershed of the Watts River, and a copy of his report was published in one of the Melbourne newspapers. It is, I believe, now admitted that the gum-trees of this district are the highest trees yet found in the world, surpassing altogether those world-famed productions of California, which have for a while been regarded as the kings of the forest. I believe I am right in asserting that no other measured trunk has been found equal in length to that above recorded. I reprint, in Appendix (No. 1), a copy of the official report made on the subject.

At Melbourne I sold my horse and saddle for £3 10s. less than I had given for them, and I thought that I had made my journey with sufficient economy.

CHAPTER VII.

I WILL now speak of the disposition of waste or crown lands in Victoria. In doing so it will be my chief object to explain the terms on which land can at present be bought, or hired, from the local authorities who represent the Crown generally in the colonies. The still unalienated lands of Australia—by which term is included the great bulk of the Australian continent—did belong to the British Crown till the period at which the colonies commenced the task of self-government. Then each colony took possession of its own land, relieving the Crown—or in other words the tax-payers of Great Britain—of the expense of colonial government in return for that concession. From that time the existing governments of the day have administered the land as trustees for the people of the colonies in conformity,— or, as some allege, not always in conformity,—with the land laws as passed by the different colonial parliaments.

That is, I think, after a rough fashion a correct statement of the manner in which the question of the disposition of Australian lands has been treated. But the subject is one full of complications, and for its thorough understanding demands the close study of some British Acts of Parliament, and of very many colonial land laws. I am aware of no general British Act of Parliament regulating the sale of waste lands in Australia, prior to that passed on June 22nd, 1842. By that Act the power of the Crown to alienate the lands was limited,—or I might almost say abrogated. With certain exceptions made on behalf of the public service, "the Crown shall not alienate these lands, unless by way of sale, nor unless such sales be conducted in the manner and according to the regulations hereinafter prescribed." Previously to that date, grants had been made at the discretion of the Crown or of the governor, and sales had been made either by auction, or at fixed price,—generally 20*s.* an acre, —in accordance with the same discretion. But long before 1842, a great interest had grown up in Australia, which, though certainly dependent on the land, did not require its alienation ;—which was indeed in its effects altogether opposed to its alienation. In 1803, Captain Macarthur, who had been employed as a soldier in New South Wales, first proposed to the government the importation of sheep and the growth of wool. If the government would grant the land, then absolutely useless, he would, at his own risk, import the sheep. Grants of land were made to Macarthur, and his scheme was pre-eminently successful. There may be a doubt whom we should regard as the first discoverer of gold in Australia, but there is no doubt that we are indebted to Captain Macarthur for the great staple of that country,—for that which was its staple before men had dreamed of Australian gold,—and for that which probably will be its chief staple again, when gold shall have either been worked out, or, as is more probable, shall have become less valuable than wool. Captain Macarthur at first asked, not for possession of land, but for "permission to occupy a sufficient tract of unoccupied lands to feed his flocks."

Mr. William Campbell, of the Legislative Council of Victoria, in an indignant protest published by him against the legislation of his colony in regard of land, thus describes the commencement of those pastoral leases by which squatters first held their somewhat precarious property :

"Others," he says, "followed his "—Captain Macarthur's—"example; the lands were lying waste; the government very wisely encouraged their occupation, and licensed any free and respectable person who desired to occupy them. Commissioners were appointed to manage these waste lands, and the occupants voluntarily paid an assessment to defray the commissioners' expenses, and that of the police under their direction ;—so that their occupation might not cost the government anything. But in the course of time, when nearly all the lands within a penetrable distance were occupied, great evils were experienced from the arbitrary acts of these functionaries, who assumed great power in defining the extent of runs by lessening one run in order to enlarge another. They were accused of receiving bribes, and of acting very unfairly between man and man. The occupants were powerless against the government, as they had only an annual licence. They could not be otherwise than dissatisfied. They required a better tenure to secure them against the irresponsible acts of an arbitrary governor and his needy subordinates. They agitated their grievances, and ultimately obtained an equitable title to a lease upon definite terms, —with a preferable right to purchase at a fair value. They obtained that title through an Act of Parliament,"—an act, that is, of the Imperial Parliament,—" and an Order of Her Majesty in Council. They were grateful for that boon granted to them, and were encouraged to improve their property under the fullest confidence that the promise of the Queen under the sanction of the Imperial Parliament would be held sacred. In this, however, they have been much disappointed ; as her Majesty's representative in Victoria violated that promise, by refusing to give the occupant of crown lands the stipulated pre-emptive right, and otherwise illegally disposed of such lands to their prejudice."

The work from which I quote was published as long ago as 1855, at which time Mr. Campbell represented very accurately the state of the Australian squatter's mind. That mind has been in no degree altered since. As Mr. Campbell and the squatters felt then, Mr. Campbell and the squatters feel now. In the above passage Mr. Campbell speaks of the squatting interest of the Australian continent generally. When the Order in Council above referred to was made, both Victoria and Queensland—under the names of Port Phillip and Moreton Bay—were parts of the great colony of New South Wales, and the order, therefore, was supposed to govern the pastoral interest of the whole territory now comprised in these three colonies. But the edge of Mr. Campbell's sword is specially sharpened against Mr. La Trobe, the first governor of Victoria, who was thought by him to have violated that Order in Council on behalf of the small farmers or free-selecters ; and the swords of the Victorian squatters generally have been sharpened against the Victorian legislatures since Mr. La Trobe's days on the same ground,—under a biting, burning, overwhelming con-viction, not only that their interests, but also that their rights, have been sacrificed to a thirst for popularity. As

Mr. La Trobe was supposed, by the squatters, to have been unjust in order that he might propitiate the growing numbers of the agricultural interest as opposed to the pastoral interest, so succeeding legislators and succeeding cabinets have been supposed to be unjust in order that they might obtain the votes of the people. Indignation is the general tone of the Australian squatter's mind, and especially of the Victorian squatter's mind ;—indignation such as glowed in the bosom of the old Duke of Newcastle when he asked whether he might not do as he liked with his own; that indignation which the aristocrat feels all the world over when he dreads that his heels will be wounded by the clouted toe of the aggressive peasant. In the old country men are reticent, and the indignation is expressed only among peers in fortune and in misfortune. When doors are closed, and the claret circulates, and all the company are azure blue, men lapped in luxury, and so secure in their possessions that they are content to hold them though giving but two per cent. for their capital, mourn together painfully, and with feigned horrors speculate on the coming of an imaginary chaos. Among the squatters of Australia the spirit of the men is the same, but the lamentations are loud and public. In both countries they who lament are the rich ones of the earth. In both countries real wealth has made itself secure, having the power which wealth always possesses of fortifying itself against aggression ; and in both cases the basis of that wealth is the possession of land.

Mr. Campbell, I think, makes out his case,—as I intend to endeavour to explain. He and the other squatters were unjustly used;—were illegally deprived of their rights, I would say, were it not that the deprivation was effected by law. I conceive it to be impossible to examine the matter without coming to the conclusion that the squatters, at any rate in Victoria, were barred by the colonial government and colonial legislature from entering in upon certain privileges promised to them by a British Order in Council founded on an Act of the British Parliament,—in full confidence upon which promises they had expended their energies and their money. But a man may be defrauded of a portion of his gains and still have so much left to him as to induce an outside observer to think that the country in which he has been able to accumulate so much so quickly, and to conserve so vast a proportion of what he has accumulated, has been a blessed country to him. Such I conceive to be the condition of the Victorian squatter,—of the man who was a squatter but is now a huge territorial landowner. He has been injured. But he has been too great to be much affected by such injury; and in spite of governors, in spite of laws, in spite of would-be-popular cabinet ministers and tribes of voters, he rides triumphant on the top of the tide.

I have alluded to the law of 1842, passed by the British Parliament in reference to Australian lands, as barring the power of the Crown to give away the crown lands at its pleasure, or to sell them except in accordance with certain fixed rules. I have also alluded to a further Act of the Imperial Parliament and to an Order in Council founded upon it, as being the basis on which the Australian squatters generally, and especially those of Victoria, rested for that security which they think has been denied to them. This Act bears date 28th August, 1846, the Order in Council 9th March, 1847,—and they provide especially for the lease of lands in New South Wales. They state the terms on which squatters will be allowed to run their flocks on the public unalienated lands in that colony, which then included both the Victoria and the Queensland of the present day.

This Order, which had and has all the strength of an Act of Parliament, having been issued in conformity with the express injunctions of an Act of Parliament, divides the public lands into three classes—a settled district, an intermediate district, and an unsettled district, and it describes, as accurately as it can do, by the names of towns, counties, and rivers, the boundaries of each. Our concern at present is with the unsettled districts, over which, more extensively from year to year, the Australian wool-growers run their flocks of sheep. The settled districts consisted chiefly of lands lying contiguous to towns or townships, and did not much concern the squatter. The intermediate districts were wider, and did concern the squatter,—but as to them he

makes no complaint. The Order in Council enacted that
in using such land he should practically have no more
than one year's tenure. If he chose to occupy such land
with his sheep,—and these lands were so occupied almost
exclusively,—he did so with the knowledge that any portion
of them might be thrown open to sale at a year's notice.
They were thrown open for sale, and have been purchased,
chiefly by the squatters themselves. In regard to the
unsettled districts it stipulates that the squatters shall have
a lease of fourteen years, that they shall pay a rental calcu-
lated at the rate of £2 10s. per thousand sheep for such a
number as the run may by survey be computed to be able
to carry, that during their leases and at the end of their
leases they shall have a "pre-emptive" right of purchase at
some price not less than 20s. an acre, and that " during the
continuance of any lease of lands occupied as a run, the
same shall not be open to purchase by any other person or
persons except the lessee thereof." The governor, however,
has reserved to him the power of selling or otherwise disposing of any special portion of land, the sale of which, or alienation of which by other means, may be required for the
public good. It can be sold, for instance, if wanted for a
village, for a railway, for a church or school, for a mine,
" or for any other purpose of public defence, safety, utility,
convenience, or enjoyment, or for otherwise facilitating the
improvement and settlement of the colony." " Hinc illæ
lachrymæ." These words are very wide,—and from the
extreme latitude given to them, or rather imposed on them,
by governors, colonial cabinet ministers, and legislators have
come the wailings and moanings of which Mr. Campbell
eighteen years since was the eloquent expositor, and which
are still heard at large through the colony.

I think that no man of common sense, who understands
the ordinary meaning of words, can doubt that the Order in
Council intended to defend the lands leased to the squatters
from all sale except when special plots were required for
special purposes. It was not intended that the land should
be thrown open to sale generally, in order that the improvement and settlement of the colony might be facilitated by

such proceeding. If so, why all these words? If so, why defend the squatters at all from the aggression of purchasers by a special Act of Parliament and a special Order in Council? The Act of 1846, and the Order in Council founded on it, may have been injudicious in conferring privileges with too open a hand upon the squatters. I think myself that such was the case. But the favours were conferred; and in any further operations either of the imperial or colonial parliaments the rights so given should have been regarded as far as the vested interests of the existing holders were concerned. It was surely a quibble to say that any governor,—as long as the governors were the responsible agents,—or any land minister when ministers were responsible,—could sell these lands without doing violence to the Order in Council, because they were empowered to do so by the clause in reference to the improvement and settlement of the colony.

But this was done. The lands were put up to sale, because, as was asserted, townships would be beneficial, and it was expedient that there should be land to be had for agricultural purposes in the neighbourhood of townships. My sympathies are all on behalf of the townships and the agricultural lands. But a bargain is a bargain, and a law is a law; and one's sense of justice is offended by any escape from a bargain or from a law by a verbal quibble. The nature of the quibble, and the ease with which an Act of Parliament may be thrown open to a coach and horses, is made ludicrously apparent by a legal opinion which the squatters got from our side of the water. They were much enraged, and determined to defend themselves, if there could be any defence, in the courts of law. So they sent home for an opinion to no less a person and no less a lawyer than our late Lord Chancellor, who was then Mr. Roundell Palmer. Probably the opinion of no English lawyer on such a subject would carry more confidence than his. Mr. Palmer's opinion was as follows:—

"I am of opinion that Mr. Forlonge "—Mr. Forlonge's case having been that which was chosen for reference—"has a clear and indisputable right to the leases; but inasmuch as they are to be granted by the authority of the governor, who represents the Crown, and no form of judicial proceeding against the governor is provided by the Act of Parliament, or the regulations, I do not think he has a specific remedy to compel the execution of such leases. At present, however, he has a complete equitable title, which the courts of justice in the colony would, I conceive, be bound and authorised to recognise, and to protest against any illegal encroachments, whether by the executive government or by private persons.

"I am clearly of opinion that neither of the sections referred to gives the governor power to withdraw any part of the runs in question—assuming, as I do, that no forfeiture has taken place—for the purposes of sale to private persons.

"I think Mr. Forlonge will be entitled to the right of pre-emption under sixth section.

"There is no course open for Mr. Forlonge, that I am aware of, except to appeal to the courts of justice in case of any illegal disturbance of his possessions.

"ROUNDELL PALMER.

"*Lincoln's Inn, 26th July*, 1853."

From this I think it will be manifest that, though Mr. Palmer held a strong opinion on Mr. Forlonge's rights, he was very far from being assured of Mr. Forlonge's power to enforce those rights. There can be no doubt of Mr. Forlonge's rights, and as little that he was not able to enforce them.

Mr. Campbell quotes with evident glee another opinion equally in his favour, and that from an enemy,—and, as it happens, from a person almost as great in the world as our late Lord Chancellor, namely, from our late Chancellor of the Exchequer. But he appeals to Mr. Lowe as to an enemy, and shows what evidence he can adduce to support his own views even from a foe. Mr. Lowe, when a colonist, was supposed to be inimical to the views of the squatters, and disapproved of the passing of the Act of 1846 and the Order in Council founded upon it. From an address which he made in 1847, Mr. Campbell quotes the following passage :—" Once grant these leases, and beyond the settled districts there will be no land to be sold. The lessees will have a right to hold these lands till some one will give £1 an acre for them. These leases cannot be sold, mortgaged, or sublet. Be the capabilities of these lands what they may, they are to be sheep-walks for ever." It was clearly Mr.

Lowe's opinion, when he spoke those words, that the squatters would be protected by the Order in Council against disturbance from purchasers, and that they would enjoy the right of pre-emption themselves if that Order were made. But the opinions held by Mr. Lowe as a politician, and expressed by Mr. Roundell Palmer as a lawyer, have been of no avail. The Order in Council was disregarded, and the free-selecters were let in upon the lands of the squatters.

I doubt much whether it will now be worth the while of any ordinary English reader to trouble himself with these matters. The chief of the lands of Victoria have settled themselves down into the hands of undoubted owners,—and as to what remains, the present law, though it may be arbitrary, is clear. Mr. Campbell and his associate squatters cannot now gain anything, and are as little likely to lose anything, by the future doings of the colonial legislature. Lord Selborne's opinion and Mr. Lowe's oratory are equally inefficacious. The thing is a thing completed. But it is impossible to understand the completion without looking back to the manner in which it was accomplished. In the Australian colonies there is growing up a rich landed aristocracy, already surrounding itself with all the feelings which attach to land in the old country. Captain Macarthur, with his first importation of sheep, might be said to be the creator of this condition of things, were it not that it is a condition peculiarly conformable to the English mind in general, so that it was in truth created to hand before Captain Macarthur ever owned a sheep. It is clear that such feelings would be fostered and brought into prominence by a pastoral and therefore patriarchal life. Squatter added himself to squatter, often suffering much, sometimes going quite to the wall, struggling frequently with untoward circumstances, —with insufficient capital, with clever and greedy merchants, with insolent servants, with unforeseen causes of decay among his flocks,—sometimes with ill-conduct, idleness, profligacy, and extravagance on his own part ; but his lot, on the whole, was a blessed lot, and he prospered marvellously. For a while it did seem as though the whole country would fall into his hands, and that the people of

G

Australia would consist of squatters and their servants.
Very much has been said, and is repeated from day to day,
of what is due to the squatters as the pioneers of Australian
civilisation.   I do not think very much of the claim.   When
a man encounters danger manifestly for the sake of others,
—that knowledge may grow and science progress, and the
world be opened to new-comers, as did such men as Colum-
bus and Cook, as many Australian explorers did, as Living-
stone was doing till he died the other day in the doing of it,
—he is entitled to public recognition and honour.   But he
can hardly with justice put forward the same claim because
he seeks fortune for himself in stormy paths.   He probably
counts his chances, and, seeing personal security with ten
per cent. at home, with forty per cent. and not improbable
annihilation at the hands of a savage at the Antipodes,
chooses forty per cent. and the Antipodes with his eyes
open.   I admire his courage, and applaud his decision.
But I cannot admit his claim as a great public benefactor,
because he has thriven and others have followed him.   He
has his reward.   It is the reward which honest, energetic
men should seek.   But I have heard the Australian squatter,
when discussing these matters, continually assert that he and
his interests should be especially regarded, because he has
been the pioneer of the country.   He has been the pioneer
of his own fortune ; and I have been rejoiced to find how
often that fortune has been noble and even princely.

The Order in Council, of which I have spoken, was clearly
made in the interests of the squatters, and was therefore, of
course, objectionable to the anti-squatting interests.   In my
own opinion it was not judicious.   If followed to the letter
it would, as Mr. Lowe said, have barred the land against
new-comers, and have perpetuated wool-growing upon soil
adapted for purposes more beneficial to mankind at large.
I do not think that there was any just claim at the time on
the part of the squatters to such favours as were conferred
upon them.   The first object of the mother country, or of
those to whose hands were confided for the time the duty of
legislating for the colonies, was to prepare homes for the
increasing hordes of colonists.   The wool-growers had spread

themselves over lands which did not belong to them, and which they occupied—no doubt with proper sanction—as waste lands. Three acres to a sheep, which sheep would produce annually about 5s. worth of wool, may be taken as a fair statement of the condition of their affairs. As long as land could be converted to no better purpose it was well that it should serve this purpose. As far as we can see at present, a very large proportion of the lands of Australia can be made to serve no better purpose. It is doubtless a fact that Australia first grew to prosperity by means of wool. At the present moment, in the very midst of the pride which she feels in her gold-fields, I put more confidence in her wool than I do in her gold. I look upon the wool-growers of Australia as her aristocracy, her gentry, her strong men, her backbone. But, in managing the affairs of this world, I do not like the theory of giving to those who have got much, and taking away from those who have got nothing. If in 1847 the general welfare of the colonists demanded that the lands of the colony should be thrown open to general sale, there was certainly nothing specially due to the squatters which should have interfered with such a policy.

It must be remembered that a system of leases to the squatters was quite compatible with a system of free-selection and open sale, that such a combination is now the law, with various modified circumstances, in the different Australian colonies, and that under it the squatters have grown rich and thriven,—unless when shut out from success by other circumstances, such as want of capital. The free-selecter will not select land serviceable only for pastoral purposes, or will ruin himself at once if he do so. He selects patches of land, and leaves the wild boundless prairies to the squatter. No doubt in Victoria the land has been bought up very much more extensively than in the other colonies ; but the history of these sales proves two points, both of which militate against the squatter's plaintive view of the matter. It shows that very much of the land was fit for higher than pastoral purposes, and that therefore the adapting of it to such higher purposes was proper. And it shows also that the prosperity of the squatters had not been seriously damaged, as they them-

selves have been the great purchasers of land from one end
of the colony to the other.

The Act of Parliament of 1846, and the Order in Council
of the following year, were surely issued in a spirit of
unnecessary tenderness for the squatter. The result of this
tenderness was disobedience to their spirit. The colony of
Victoria, whether by its governor or subsequently by its
own parliament, upset the Order in Council. Our great
English lawyer declared very plainly the strength of Mr.
Forlonge's undoubted legal rights. But Mr. Forlonge and
his brethren did not get their legal rights. They only got
what should have been their rights. That such a course has
in the long run been greatly for the advantage of the squatters will hardly be doubted by a looker-on from a distance.
No law can render permanent injustice endurable to a community. As it is the squatters hold their own, and can hold
it with a tight hand. The public feeling that if thay have
had some favour shown them they have also had some dis-
favour, gives them strength. Nothing ruins so surely as
uninterrupted and partial privileges. Nothing strengthens
so healthily as bearable wrongs. The Victorian squatter has
suffered no more than parental scourges.

But indeed the Victorian squatter has almost ceased to
exist,—for the squatter, properly so called, is he who runs
his flocks upon crown lands. The Victorian wool-grower
has generally purchased his run and owns it in fee,—as does
also the Victorian grazier, who is as great a man as the wool-
grower. Were I to attempt to describe the manner in
which the lands of the colony have been purchased, I might
devote a volume to the subject, and years to the study of it
before I could write the volume. It seems to have been
the object of the legislature to prevent the absorption of
large tracts of land by great capitalists, and to create a
yeomanry possessing freeholds. The result has been directly
opposite to the intended purpose. The yeomanry, such as
it is, can hardly as yet be regarded as a prosperous people.
Their lands pass frequently from hand to hand. But, on
the other hand, a strong race of territorial magnates has
created itself, so wealthy and so extensive that the political

power of the country is inefficacious against them. Laws have been passed with the express intention of keeping the lands out of the squatters' hands. Nevertheless the squatters have bought the lands. There have been subterfuges, chicanery, bribery, the driving of many coaches through many Acts of Parliament. The squatters no doubt have been subjected to cruel ill-usage by a tribe of land-sharks. Men have lived and made fortunes by threatening to bid for land against the squatters, unless paid exorbitantly for bidding on their behalf. The poor squatters have bled at all pores. But they have had the blood to give, and now they own the land.

I have said that the lands of Victoria have been for the most part sold. This, no doubt, is the case in regard to the colony at large, and the traveller as he travels through the better-known and better-cultivated parts of it,—especially those western regions which were at one time called Australia Felix,—will find that he passes from one property to another, much in the same fashion as he will do at home. But Victoria is a large place, and there is still very much land open for purchase from the government. The existing law under which land can be bought is as follows :—

The intending purchaser, having selected his block of land, which must not exceed half a square mile, or 320 acres, applies for a licence to occupy it for three years as a tenant at a rent of 2s. an acre. The law states that this licence, may be granted by the governor, but in fact the power rests with a member of the cabinet, who is called the Commissioner of Lands. One half-year's rent must be paid in advance, and for the three years he continues to pay at the rate of 2s. an acre. At the end of the three years, provided the selecter shall then have fenced his land and have cultivated one-tenth of it, he can become the freeholder by paying 14s. an acre down, or he can continue to pay a rental for seven years at the rate of 2s. an acre, at the end of which time the land will be his. He thus, in fact, pays a rental of 2s. an acre for ten years, and then becomes the owner of the land without further purchase-money. The terms are very easy, and it is certain that there is still land to be bought in Victoria on those terms, which is worth much more than

the money required for it. But there are two difficulties in
the way of the free-selecter;—he may not know how to
choose his land, and, when he has made his choice, his
application may be unsuccessful.

That many men choose amiss in this colony and others
is too true. They are in a hurry for possession. They do
not know the circumstances of the country or district which
affect the land,—such as the prevaience of drought, the
prevalence of rust in the wheat, the difficulty of finding a
market, the cost of labour, and the like. They have no
friend capable of giving counsel, or, more probably, they
have a friend who has some interest of his own in the
transaction. One's heart bleeds at hearing of the unfortunate
purchases sometimes made by new-comers, and one thinks
of Cairo and Martin Chuzzlewit. As to that want of success in the application, I feel that I tread on somewhat
delicate ground in alluding to it. One supposes naturally
that if the applicant comply with all the required stipula-
tions and have his money in his hands, he will be successful
as a matter of course. Why not? And if he be not so, on
what ground and in whose bosom shall rest the decision of
granting this application and refusing that? I must say
that if there be no other ground than that of fitness,—if
nothing else than the character and means of the applicant
be considered in granting and refusing these applications,—
the minister of the day who happens to be Commissioner of
Lands is at the same time the best and the worst abused
man in the colony. It is asserted everywhere that the sales
of land are effected with direct reference to political support, and that it would be impossible for a land minister to
carry on his work in the colony on any other basis. This
system of political corruption, of using the patronage and
discretion of the government to bolster up the power of the
government, from which we are only now emerging at home,
is in truth so rampant in Victoria that honest men,—in no
wise concerned in the matter, but who have become used
to it by daily observation,—have learned to think that it is
a necessary part of government. Remembering how offices
in England were given away in my own time, how some

are given still, solely on the score of political subserviency, I do not feel justified in expressing great indignation at this practice in the colonies. It will doubtless pass away. But the wrongful exercise of patronage in a young colony is a much smaller fault than an unjust political manipulation in the distribution of public lands.

It is especially stipulated by the Victorian land law that no one person, either in his own name or that of another, shall select and purchase above 320 acres,—the object being to prevent the accumulation of large landed estates. But the clause has been constantly set at nought. If I buy one section for myself, and nine other adjacent sections through the friendly assistance of nine " dummies," as they are called, how can a land commissioner, with a whole colony on his hands, discern the fraud? And if I be true to the party which have put him into office, why should he wish to discern it? Without a doubt the squatters themselves, who are loud against the lawlessness of Victorian legislation, have been the most constant in evading the laws. Their success makes it impossible for the stranger to condole with their wrongs. At the end of this volume, as an appendix, will be found a digest of the present land laws of Victoria, as far as they refer to free-selection. This digest is taken from MacPhaile's Australian Squatting Directory.

They who are still really squatters in Victoria,—who run their sheep on public lands, and not on their own,—now pay a pastoral rent of 8d. a sheep, or £33 6s. 8d. per thousand. The old rental as fixed by the Order in Council in 1847 was £2 10s. per thousand. The rental at present paid is four times higher than that collected in either of the other Australian colonies. But the bulk of the Victorian wool is grown by men who own the land which produces it.

I found that the system of landlord and tenant—with which we are so familiar at home as almost to have conceived the idea that land cannot be occupied on any other system—does prevail in certain parts of Victoria. I visited a district in which large wheat farms were held by tenants, and I was told of rents varying from 5s. to 15s. an acre.

But it did not appear that the tenant-farmers were a prosperous class, or that the letting of land was popular among
landowners.   In some instances a whole property is let with
the stock upon it, and I have heard of as much as £10,000
a year being paid for a sheep-run with the use of the sheep
on it ; but in speaking of the letting of land of course I do
not allude to such cases as this.   The small tenant-farmer
in the colonies is seldom a man of means.   Did he possess
capital he would buy his farm.   Not possessing capital he
cannot pay his rent when bad years come ;—and it almost
seemed that, as far as the produce of wheat went, bad years
were as common as good years in Victoria.   The ground
produced enormously,—with most generous vigour, I must
say, considering how little is restored to it.   But the climate
is uncertain, and the disease called the rust is pernicious.
One gentleman, who owned a large tract of corn-bearing
land, assured me that he much preferred selling portions of
his property, even though the purchase-money were left on
mortgage, to accepting a promise of yearly rent for the use
of his land.

I have said that the public lands are alienated in fee for a
rental of 2s. an acre for ten years, and that tenant-farmers
pay rents varying from 5s. to 15s. an acre,—the payment of
which for any number of years gives, of course, no title to
possession.   It is presumed that the reader will understand
that the public, or crown, lands spoken of are uncultivated,
unfenced, and probably covered with timber.   The farm
lands let for the higher rentals named have been brought
into cultivation, have been farmed, and are supposed to be
capable of bearing corn.

CHAPTER VIII.

LADIES AND GENTLEMEN.

A WRITER attempting to describe England, and capable of doing so, would fill those chapters with the strongest interest in which he painted the various forms of English country life. He would know, and he would teach his readers, that the English character, with its faults and virtues, its prejudices and steadfastness, can be better studied in the mansions of noblemen, in country-houses, in parsonages, in farms, and small meaningless towns, than in the great cities, devoted as is London to politics and gaiety, or as are Glasgow, Manchester, Birmingham, and others like them, to manufactures and commerce. I doubt whether this be so in any other country. France has many aspects, but the Parisian aspect is more French than any other. Italy is to be seen only in her cities. In the United States the towns altogether overrule and subdue the country, so that the traveller who visits America under the most favourable circumstances rarely sees aught of her corn-fields and pastures, except in passing from one great centre of population to another. But the visitors to England who have not sojourned at a country-house, whether it be squire's, parson's, or farmer's, have not seen the most English phase of the country.

The same form and fashion of life is repeating itself in the Australian colonies. The race of farmers, such as are our own well-to-do farmers at home, does not, indeed, exist. The clergy are scattered at long distances, and hardly as yet form a distinctive social class,—probably never will do so as they do in England, and in England only. But the country gentlemen, almost all of whom were originally squatters, have fixed their homes about the colony, and have built their houses,—not exactly after the English fashion in regard to architecture, because the climate is of a different nature, —but with the English appurtenances of substantial comfort, with many rooms, with gardens, outhouses, and lawns, and with sweeping roads leading through timbered parks to the retired abode of the rural magistrate who owns the property. The visitor to Australia, who goes there under favourable auspices, will as surely find himself pressed to make his home at such country houses, as will the stranger in the United States be asked to enjoy the luxurious hospitality of her rich citizens, either in city mansions or in suburban villas. And such a one, if he have time on his hands, and can dally with weeks in idleness, may pass from station to station,—from one gentleman's house to another,—till he will hardly know who has sent him on, or on what ground he bases his claim to the hospitality of his new friends.

There is perhaps more of this in Victoria than in the other colonies, because the country gentlemen have more thoroughly established their fortunes there than elsewhere ; but the same feeling prevails throughout Australia, and the same mode of life. They who rise to the top of the tree,—or, in other words, the gentry, if I may use a phrase which is somewhat invidious, but which will be better understood than any other,—seek to establish country houses for themselves ; and homesteads of this class have sprung up with incredible rapidity. Nothing, I think, so clearly declares the wealth of the colony—which is not yet forty years old— as the solidity of her country life. When the stranger asks whence came these country gentlemen, whom he sees occasionally at the clubs and dinner-tables in Melbourne, exactly as he finds those in England up in London during the winter frosts, or in the month of May, he is invariably told that they or their fathers made their own fortunes. This man and that and the other came over perhaps from Tasmania, in the early days, joint owners of a small flock of sheep. They generally claim to have suffered every adversity with which

Providence and unjust legislators could inflict a wretched victim; and, as the result, each owns so many thousand horned cattle, so many tens of thousand sheep, so many square miles of country, and so many thousands a year. Most of them have, I think, originally come out of Scotland. When you hear an absent acquaintance spoken of as "Mac," you will not at all know who is meant, but you may safely conclude that it is some prosperous individual. Some were butchers, drovers, or shepherds themselves but a few years since. But they now form an established aristocracy, with very conservative feelings, and are quickly becoming as firm a country party as that which is formed by our squirearchy at home.

I have spoken of country life in New South Wales without reserve, because the small establishment which I described belongs to my own son. In Victoria I visited many houses of infinitely greater pretension, but I fear to speak of any one in particular lest I should commit that great sin,—not always avoided as scrupulously as it should be by travelling authors,—of putting some kind host into a book, with his wife, family, kitchen and cellars. And yet, if it be possible, I would fain let English readers know what these houses are, and of what nature is the life contained in them. They are generally less remote from towns than are the habitations of squatters in the other colonies,—the towns being more numerous, and the roads more formed. The buildings themselves are generally of two stories,—always having the tropical addition of a verandah, but not erected in that straggling, many-roofed, one-storied fashion which is common to tropical and semi-tropical countries. I like those straggling many-roofed nests of cottages which are common in Queensland and New South Wales. They betoken a gradually increasing prosperity. The squatter builds first a wooden hut which ultimately becomes his kitchen, then a wooden sitting-room and bedroom near to it; then a bigger sitting-room with two small bedrooms, still of wood,—and so on. But when he has realised to himself the fact that he is a rich man he rushes into brick and mortar or stone, and erects a European country house,—

with the addition of a wide verandah. This has been done now very generally by the landowners of Victoria. But still the place has rarely all the finished comfort, the easy grace, coming from long habit, which belong to our country seats at home. There is a roughness and a heaviness about it, a want of completion about the gardens, of neatness about the paths, and of close-shorn trimness about the plots and lawns, which strikes the beholder at once, and declares that though the likeness be there, it exists with a difference.

This difference is caused chiefly by the dearness of labour, a fact which influences not only the outside of the Victorian gentleman's house, but also every part of his establishment. Let his means be what they may, he never has the retinue of servants which is to be found in an ordinary English household. The high rate of wages and the difficulty of getting persons to accept these high rates for any considerable number of months together, cause even the wealthy to dispense with much of that attendance which is often considered indispensable at home even among families that are not wealthy. On the other hand, certain luxuries are common among Australian families, which few among us can enjoy without stint. He who has a carriage and horses at home is supposed to be a rich man. If a gentleman have daughters fond of riding, he will perhaps have one horse for two girls. Young men can hardly hunt unless their fathers be wealthy. But horses on an Australian station are as common as blackberries on English hedges, and the possession of a carriage and pair of horses is as much a matter of course as the possession of a pair of boots. But horses are cheap and servants are dear in Victoria.

I have spoken of sweeping roads through timbered parks. It must not, however, be conceived that I speak of parks such as those which are the glory of our English magnates. The Australian park is hitherto much as nature fashioned it. The trees are the gum-trees which the present resident or his father found there when he first drove his sheep on the pastures which had never yet known the foot of a white man. The grasses round his house he may gradually have changed, and have extirpated those indigenous to the soil by the use of English seeds. The road will probably be somewhat rough, and the fences which divide the paddocks still rougher. He is now a rich man, but he is rich because in all his expenditure he has thought more of a return for his capital than of the adornment of his place. He calls his park a paddock, and he has thought only of the welfare of his stock. But, nevertheless, there is that beauty about it which trees and grass, with the sky above them, always produce. And the territory is large and spacious, and all the magnificence of ownership is there. The man drives for miles through his own land. He has fortified himself on all sides against free-selecters. All those who frequent the place are his servants or his guests, and of every stranger whom he may see within miles of his house he is entitled to ask why he is there. He exercises a wide hospitality to the poor and the rich, and he is an aristocrat.

I imagine that the life of the Victorian landowner is very much as was that of the English country gentleman a century or a century and a half ago. In those days roads in England were very bad, so that it was a work of trouble to get from one house to another, a distance of twenty miles. Country houses of pretension were not numerous as they are now, and they who owned the halls and granges scattered through the counties rarely moved from their homes. There was great plenty, but of that finished luxury which is now as common in the country as in the capital, there was but little. Roast beef—or in winter powdered beef—and October ale were the fare. The men were fond of sport, but they did not go far afield for it as they do now, hunting in the shires, shooting on the moors, and fishing on all lakes and rivers. They shot over their own lands, and hunted over their own land and that of a few neighbours who would join them. The ladies stayed at home and looked after the house, and much that is now trusted to domestics and stewards was done by the mistress and her daughters, or by the master and his sons. The owners of these country houses were Tories, aristocrats, proud gentlemen; but they were not fine gentlemen, nor, for the most part, were they gentlemen of fine tastes in art or literature. We know them very well from plays and novels,—and know something of them too from history, as history has of late been written. The ladies' dresses, the books, the equipages, the wines, the kitchens, which are now found in English country houses, were in those days known only in the metropolis, or at the castle of some almost royal nobleman. As were country houses and country life then in England, plentiful, proud, prejudiced, given to hospitality, impatient of contradiction, not highly lettered, healthy, industrious, careful of the main chance, thoughtful of the future, and, above all, conscious— perhaps a little too conscious—of their own importance, so now is the house and so is the life of the country gentleman in Australia. And as Justice Shallow in times still farther distant was ever anxious as to the price of a good yoke of bullocks or a score of ewes, so does the Australian country gentleman never omit his solicitude concerning those things which have made him what he is. The value of beef in the Melbourne market, and of wool at London, are continually in his thoughts, and as continually on his tongue, even though he may have reached that stage of prosperity which cannot be much affected by the transient rise or fall of prices. He has not at any rate reached that condition,—be it good or bad,—which enables the English country gentle- man to drop all outward show of solicitude for the trade in which he is embarked, the trade namely of living upon his land, and to pursue the unruffled tenor of his way as though all good things came to him and were sure to come to him like manna from heaven. The Victorian wool-grower or grazier will be sure to tell you, if you visit him in his own home, what has been his produce of wool, and what prices he has realised for it,—and will take you to his washpool, if he wash his sheep before shearing, and to his wool-shed; or he will show you his Durhams and Herefords, and boast how he has led the markets. Out of the full heart the mouth speaks. He has made himself what he is by his sheep and his oxen, and the sheep and the oxen are still dear to him. His grandson or great-grandson will probably be as outwardly indifferent as an English country gentleman, who is no more given to talk of his rents than a banker is of his profits, and who is concerned wholly, perhaps with his hounds, perhaps with his library, perhaps with his politics, or perhaps with his cook.

Out-of-door sports do not form so prominent a part of country life in the colonies us they do at home, partly because there are not so many idle men, and partly because there has not been as yet so great an expenditure of money with the view of creating sport. As years pass on both these causes will vanish. The idle men will be forthcoming, and game, brought from England, Scotland, and Ireland, will be naturalised in the country. Hares in Victoria will be, I hope, not quite so plentiful as rabbits. There are deer already in the country, and they will soon abound with that prolific increase which seems to attend all animals brought from the old country to these colonies. Duck-shooting is much practised, and ducks abound. Pheasants are already more common in parts of New Zealand than in England, though not so plentiful, and will probably become equally common in Tasmania and Victoria. I despair, however, of fox-hunting. I think it improbable that that most anomalous, most irrational, most exciting, most de-lightful, and most beneficent sport should thrive elsewhere on the world's surface than in the British Isles. None but the British and Irish farmer will bear the invasion of a troop of horsemen. None but the British or Irish sportsman can have that tenderness in preserving and that stern perse-verance in killing a little vermin, which fox-hunting re-quires. None but a British or an Irish gentleman can expend thousands in furnishing amusement for an entire county.

The fault of a country home in the Australian colonies is that it furnishes but little employment, and that its ordinary life seems to be antagonistic to industry, at any rate on the part of the visitor. The master of the house is or is not the working manager of his property. If he be so, his time is fully occupied. He is on horseback before break-fast, and seems never to slacken his labours till the evening dews have long fallen. The exclusive care of a large flock of sheep,—which includes breeding, feeding, doctoring, shearing, selling and buying, together with the hiring, feeding, inspection, and payment of a great number of by no means subservient workmen,—taxes a man's energies to the utmost. Cattle probably impose less labour, but a man will have his hands fairly full who owns three or four thousand head of cattle, who breeds them by his own judgment, and himself selects them for market. But very many squatters and graziers really manage their properties by deputy. Serviceable men have grown up in their employment, and as years creep on the real work of the run is allowed to fall from their own hands into those of superintendents and overseers. Then the country gentleman, though he still talks of "a score of ewes" as did Justice Shallow, becomes an idle man. He comes down to breakfast at nine, and is impatient for his dinner before six, thinking that the clock must be losing time. The ladies no doubt look after their houses, order lunch and dinner, and superintend the servants. But they seem to be insufficiently provided with occupations over and above these. There is a piano in every house. There are always books,—enough for reading, though not enough for literary luxury. There may be croquet out of doors. There are horses to ride; and there is the unlimited bush, with its magpies, its laughing jackasses, and its bell-birds, if you be good at walking. But there is no provision made for the passing of time. There is no period of the day at which books fall naturally into the hands of men and women. Loitering is common, and the hours too often become foes instead of friends. This is specially the case during the long evenings. I fancy that the same fault might have been found with country houses in England a hundred and fifty years ago.

Eating and drinking occupy so many of our thoughts, and contribute so much to the excitement and to the amusement of life, that I feel myself bound to say something of the Victorian country gentleman's taste. No table more plentiful or more hospitable was ever spread. Its chief distinctive feature is the similarity of the meals. The breakfast is nearly as substantial as the lunch and dinner, and between the lunch and dinner it was long before I could find out any difference. Two or three hot joints of meat and four or five dishes of vegetables, wine-decanters, and not uncommonly a teapot, are common to both of them. As regarded the time allowed, or the appetite, or that addition to appetite which greediness furnishes throughout the world, I could not ascertain that there was any distinction between the two. With us at home the cook never exerts herself,—or himself,—for lunch, and is not indeed expected to do so. The Victorian cook is equally awake all the day long. At last I perceived that at luncheon there would never be more than two puddings. At dinner the number was not limited. As a rule, gentlemen in the colonies do not sit long over their wine; and, as a rule, also,—and rules, of course, have their exceptions,—the wine is not worth a long sitting.

But these little details of which I have spoken do but form the outside skin of society, whereas the bones, the muscles, the blood, and the flesh consist of the people themselves. Whether men and women dine at five or at seven, whether they drive out regularly or irregularly, whether they hunt foxes or kangaroos, drink bad wine or good, matters little, in regard to social delights, in comparison with the character, the manners, and the gifts of the men and women themselves. In describing Victorians of the upper classes, and of the two sexes, I would say that both in their defects and their excellences they approach nearer to the American than to the British type. And in this respect the Victorian is distinct from the colonist of New South Wales, who retains more of the John-Bull attributes of the mother country than his younger and more energetic brother in the South. This is visible, I think, quite as much in the women as in the men. I am speaking now especially of those women whom on account of their education and position we should class as ladies; but the remark is equally true to all ranks of society. The maidservant in Victoria has the pertness, the independence, the mode of asserting by her manner that though she brings you up your hot water, she is just as good as you,—and a good deal better

H

if she be younger,—which is common to the American
"helps." But in Victoria, as in the States, the offensiveness
of this—for to us who are old-fashioned it is in a certain
degree offensive—is compensated by a certain intelligence
and instinctive good-sense which convinces the observer
that however much he may suffer, however heavily the young
woman may tread upon his toes, she herself has a good
time in the world. She is not degraded in her own estimation by her own employment, and has no idea of being
humble because she brings you hot water. And when we
consider that the young woman serves us for her own purposes, and not for ours, we cannot rationally condemn her.
The spirit which has made this bearing so common in the
United States,—where indeed it is hardly so universal now
as it used to be,—has grown in Victoria and has permeated
all classes. One has to look very closely before one can
track it out and trace it to be the same in the elegantly
equipped daughter of the millionaire who leads the fashion
in Melbourne and in the little housemaid; but it is the
same. The self-dependence, the early intelligence, the
absence of reverence, the contempt for all weakness,—even
feminine weakness,—the indifference to the claims of age,
the bold self-assertion, have sprung both in the one class
and in the other from the rapidity with which success in life
has been gained. The class of which I am now specially
speaking is an aristocrat class; but it is an aristocracy of
yesterday; and the creation of such an aristocracy does
away with reverence and puts audacity in its place. The
young housemaid does not shake in her shoes before you
because you have £10,000 a year, and the young lady has
no special respect for you because you are her father's old
friend. Her father and her father's friends have had their
time. It is her time now. It is for her to stand in the
middle and for them to range themselves on one side. She
will do her duty by her father and mother,—but she does it
as a superior person attending on those who are inferior.
To her grandfather and her grandmother she alludes as poor
things of the past, to whom much tenderness is due. But
the attention is paid after a fashion which seems to imply

that old folk, in the arrangements of life, should not interfere with their betters who are young. Luckily for fathers
and grandfathers in Victoria the power of the purse remains
with them, otherwise they would I fear be ciphers in the
houses that were once their own. The Australian girls and
young married women are not cruel, false, or avaricious, and
I will not call them Gonerils and Regans ; but I have seen
old men who have put me in mind of Lear.

There is a manifest difference between women who have
come out from England and those who are " colonial-born,"
which is not at all points in favour of the former. If we
are to take personal appearance as the good thing most in
request by the female sex, I think that the girls born in the
colony have the pre-eminence. As a rule they are very
pretty, having delicate sweet complexions and fine forms.
They grow quickly, and are women two years earlier in life
than are our girls,—and consequently are old women some
five years sooner. They are bright and quick, hardly as yet
thoroughly educated, as the means of thorough education
for women do not grow up in a new country very readily ;
but they have all achieved a certain amount of information
which they have at their fingers' ends. They never appear
to be stupid or ignorant,—because they are never bashful
or diffident. We do not criticise very accurately the law as
laid down to us by a pretty woman,—being thankful for any
law from bright eyes and ruby lips. Sometimes at home
we can get no law, no opinion, no rapid outflow of sweet-
sounding words,—because some modest sense of the weakness of feminine youth restrains the speech. It must be
admitted, however, that even at home this failing is less
general than it used to be.

Women, all the world over, are entitled to everything
that chivalry can give them. They should sit while men
stand. They should be served while men wait. Men
should be silent while they speak. They should be praised,
—even without desert. They should be courted,—even
when having neither wit nor beauty. They should be
worshipped,—even without love. They should be kept
harmless while men suffer. They should be kept warm

while men are cold. They should be kept safe while men
are in danger. They should be enabled to live while men
die in their defence. All this chivalry should do for women,
and should do as a matter of course. But there is a reason
for this deference. One human being does not render all
these services to another,—who cannot be more than his
equal before God,—without a cause. A man will serve a
woman, will suffer for her,—if it come to that will die for
her,—because she is weaker than he and needs protection.
Let her show herself to be as strong, let her prove by her
prowess and hardihood that the old idea of her comparative
weakness has been an error from the beginning, and the
very idea of chivalry, though it may live for awhile by the
strength of custom, must perish and die out of men's hearts.
I have often felt this in listening to the bold self-assertion
of American women,—not without a doubt whether chivalry
was needed for the protection of beings so excellent in
their own gifts, so superabundant in their own strength.
And the same thought has crept over me when I have been
among the ladies of Victoria. No doubt they demand all
that chivalry can give them. No ladies with whom I am
acquainted are more determined to enforce their rights in
that direction. But they make their claim with arms in
their hands,—at the very point of the bodkin. Stand aside
that I may pass on. Be silent that I may speak. Lay
your coat down upon the mud and perish in the
cold, lest my silken slippers be soiled in the mire. Be
wounded that I may be whole. Die, that I may live. And
for the nonce they are obeyed. That strength of custom
still prevails, and women in Victoria enjoy for a while all
that weakness gives, and all that strength gives also. But
this, I think, can only be for a day. They must choose
between the two, not only in Victoria but elsewhere. As
long as they will put up with that which is theirs on the
score of feminine weakness, they are safe. There is no
tendency on the part of men to lessen their privileges.
Whether they can make good their position in the other
direction may be doubtful. I feel sure that they cannot
long have both, and I think it unfair that they should

make such demand. For the sake of those who are to
come after me,—both men and women,—I hope that there
may be no change in the old-established fashion.

I write these words in fear and trembling, lest the ladies
of Victoria should condemn my book, and set me down as
one who had accepted and betrayed hospitality. Let them
remember all that I have conceded to them. They are
lovely, bright, quick-witted, and successful. If, having said
so much on their behalf, I venture to add a few words of
counsel, they should remember that unqualified praise is
always egregious flattery.

In speaking of men I can venture to use my pen with
greater courage, and to say what I have to say without
bating my breath. To their censure I can be deaf, and
callous to their displeasure. The Victorian old man hardly
as yet exists. Among those who are near the top of the
tree it is rare to find even those who have been born in the
other colonies. The men who have hitherto prospered best
in Australia are they who came young from the old country,
without much money, with great energy, and with a strong
conviction that fortune was to be made by industry,
sobriety, and patience. These men succeeded, and they or
their descendants are now the landed gentry of the country.
Some are dead, and their places are filled by their sons.
Some are tottering in old age, and their work is carried on
by their sons. But there are enough of them still left in
hale strength to give a tone to the entire colony. They
smack of England,—or of Scotland or Ireland, as the case
may be,—and are very different in their manners from those
younger than themselves, who have been born in Australia.
There are of course many, still young, who have come out
from England,—so many that they suffice to give a tone to
the whole social life of the colony. But every year this
becomes less so than it was the year before, and the time
will soon come in which the colonial will be stronger than
the home flavour. It is of interest to inquire whether the
race will deteriorate or become stronger by the change.

Dividing the population into two classes,—which, in
order that I may be understood, I will call the upper and

the lower class,—I speak now of that which is by far the less important as being the less numerous. As regards the masses of the men who earn their bread by their manual labour I have no doubt whatever that the born colonist is superior to the emigrant colonist,—any more than I have that the emigrant is superior to his weaker brother whom he leaves behind him. The best of our workmen go from us, and produce a race superior to themselves. The labourer born in the colonies is better educated than the man who has come from the old country, and is very much more sober. He is better fed than the labourer at home, better housed, better clothed, and is therefore more of a man. I think that any observer seeing the artisans in an Australian town, the miners on an Australian gold-field, or the shearers in an Australian wool-shed, would come to this conclusion, —and would feel that no workman should remain at home who can make himself master of a passage to the colonies. I cannot speak with the same confidence of those who are born to positions which we regard as higher than those of a daily workman. The young Australian-born "gentleman" has certain points in his favour. He who goes out from England belonging to that class has not uncommonly been sent there because he has not hitherto done very well at home. I have said that the best of our labourers emigrate ; but we certainly do not send to the colonies the best of our youth from Oxford and Cambridge, our most learned young lawyers, our cleverest engineers, or the most promising sons of our merchants and tradespeople. The young colonial scion is not called on to compete with the élite of the youth of the mother country. But in the competition to which he is called, he hardly as yet holds his own. He rarely runs into bad vices. He does not drink, or gamble, or go utterly to the dogs. But he is too often listless, unenergetic, vain, and boastful. Up to a certain age, that of advanced boyhood, he is generally clever, quick at learning what he does learn, and very often superior in general information to a boy from Harrow or from Winchester. He has more to say for himself, is less addicted to mere boyish amuse-ments, and comes out as a man at an earlier age. But he has that fault which belongs to all produce of field and garden which grows ripe too quickly. When Clara in "Philip van Artevelde" boasted that she, being of the softer sex, was privileged to grow ripe on the sunny side of the wall, she had probably not yet learned that the fruit which hangs through the autumn has the finer flavour, and can be kept till the end of winter. The colonial young man—a young man while he still should be a boy—hardly keeps the promise of his early years, and seems to lack something of that energy which grows up among us during the protracted years of our juvenility.

It is common to hear this discussed in the colonies themselves,—where the old swans are by no means disposed to look upon their cygnets as goslings. It is acknowledged, at any rate, that the boy grows out of boyhood earlier than he does in the old country. It is common to attribute the change to the climate ; and there certainly is apparent ground for doing so, as we know that puberty is attained earlier in warm than in cold countries. I do not, however, believe that the climate is accountable for the great difference which exists,—especially as there is another cause in operation which must, I think, have produced it without other cause. Hitherto the education of youths in the Australian colonies has been quick, perfunctory, and perhaps superficial. That it should have been of this kind, is so natural,—that it should gradually cease to be open to such censure as the modes of education are improved, is again so natural,—that we may be justified in looking for the decrease and gradual cessation of an evil so caused, whereas, were it attributable to the climate, any remedy for it would be beyond the reach of our energy and wisdom. We are apt, in the old country, to complain bitterly of the years which are devoted to the pursuit of limited knowledge very imperfectly mastered. At eighteen or nineteen our boys, though they have been at school for the last ten years, do not speak Latin, do not read Greek fluently, bungle in their French, and are novices at mathematics. But during the whole time they have been learning much which cannot be put into any examination paper, and which they cannot reckon up in the list of their acquirements. They may be idle, but they are rarely listless. They may dislike study, but they do not love to sit still and whistle.

Gradually there is growing up in the colonies a desire for protracted education on the part of fathers who can afford to bestow such advantage on their sons. There are universities at Sydney and Melbourne, which indeed are as yet only in their infancy in regard to numbers, but which have the means of giving, and which are intended to give, the protracted education of which I speak. Gradually they will grow into favour, and the example which they set will be followed by schools throughout the colonies. What is chiefly required on behalf of the colonial-born youth is that he should be kept a little longer from the appurtenances of manhood. He should be taught to cease to think that the prime of life has been reached at nineteen.

CHAPTER IX.

I DISLIKE the use of superlatives, especially when they are applied in eulogy; nevertheless, I feel myself bound to say that I doubt whether any country in the world has made quicker strides towards material comforts and well-being than have been effected by Victoria. She is not forty years old, all told,—going back even to the date at which Mr. Henty landed at Portland,—and she has already at her command most of the enjoyments of civilised life. Of her great city, Melbourne, I have spoken,—and of her gold-fields and that wonderful gold-town, Ballaarat ; also of the country life of her country gentlemen. But there are other matters in which she has advanced as quickly : and I must say a word of her newspapers, her general produce, her railways, her roads and coaches, her country towns, and her native wines.

With all the prejudice of a genuine Briton, I think that no country has ever yet produced newspapers equal to those of England. This fact—if it be a fact—I attribute partly to her wealth, partly to her general energy, partly to her love of fair play, but chiefly to her determination that the press shall be free. In France many of the writers of news-papers are at any rate equal in talent to their brethren among us, and, as a rule, they stand higher in public estimation. They are known by name, and they have a wider reputation. But they do not produce the same sort of article. The French newspaper is more confined than the English, and either more vapid in its obedience to authority, or more violent in its opposition. There is no catering for informa-

tion at all approaching in extensiveness to that practised by
our great metropolitan and provincial daily papers ; and the
means expended on the production of a newspaper are
infinitely less. The article when produced is readable in
regard to language and type, and has opinions of its own,
perhaps very strongly developed, as to the central political
subject of the day in France itself ; but beyond that it is
generally barren of information, and is often half filled with
extraneous matter, which might be more conveniently used
in the form of a volume. But if the French newspapers
dissatisfy us, what are we to say of those of the United
States? With a fair experience of their journals, with a
conviction favourable in general to American habits and
American institutions, with strongest feelings of social friendship for Americans whom I know and of political friendship
for Americans generally, I am bound to declare that I never
had a newspaper of the United States in my hand without
suffering during the whole time that I was reading it. The
sensational headings, spread over an amount of column
often greater than that afterwards devoted to the subject
itself, disgust and irritate. There will be a dozen such
headings in every paper, and not a scrap of news to create
sensation afterwards. The language is bombastic, vulgar,
and very frequently so faulty as to leave on the mind an
impression that the persons employed cannot generally belong to the same class as do our writers for the daily press.
Their type is bad. Their paper is bad,—and when you
have read a journal through with the greatest diligence, you
declare, as you throw it aside, that there is nothing in it
whatever. An American can give a good lecture,—much
better generally than any Englishman,—can make a good
speech, can build a good house, can cook a good dinner,
can bake good bread, can tell a good story, can write a good
book, can do, as I think, anything on earth requiring in-
tellect, energy, industry, and construction,—with this one
exception. He cannot,—at any rate as yet he has not
turned out a good newspaper.

But Victoria, with her 750,000 souls, has a good daily
newspaper,—as has also New South Wales, with her 500,000

souls. Indeed, in this respect I intend to give no priority to the one over the other, having failed to form an opinion as to which was the best. But I think that the Melbourne "Argus" and the Sydney "Morning Herald" are the best daily papers I have seen out of England. Sydney is nearly a hundred years old, and is perhaps entitled to a good news-paper; but it is remarkable that there should be such a paper as the "Argus" in a town which was a wilderness forty years since. Melbourne also has a weekly paper, the "Austra-lasian," which is as good in its way as the "Argus." Com-mon report says that as pecuniary speculations these perio-dicals have been highly successful;—but then so also is the New York "Morning Herald"!

General literature is perhaps the product which comes last from the energies of an established country. Men must eat before they can write, and all think of eating before they think of writing. Leisure, which is compatible only with fixed means of living, is necessary for the production of books. Books in these halcyon days do no doubt provide bread for the writers of them; but the man who with empty pocket attempts to begin the opening of his oyster by the production of a book, will too often have to endure almost starvation before his oyster is reached.

The production of books must follow the production of other things, and the growth of literature will be slow. Victoria, however, and the Australian colonies generally have produced many books. I cannot say that as yet their volumes are to be found crowding the shelves of European libraries. It would be odd indeed if it were so, as the country has not yet been open to European enterprise, or even to European footsteps, for a full century. I have been surprised to find not only how many books have been written in Australia, and sent home for publication,—books generally of colonial history, colonial experience, and colo-nial exploration,—which have made their mark, but also how vast a number of small volumes have issued in the colonies, from the presses of Melbourne and Sydney, which, alas! have as yet done but little either for the pockets or the fame of the writers. Very many of these little books—the majority of the great number which reached my hands—contained verse, verse that was heroic, verse that was elegiac, verse that was burlesque, verse that was amatory, and very often verse that was plaintive. I never had one of these unpretending products of ambitious souls in my hand without thinking of the hopes which were once high, so soon to be dashed to the ground,—of the grand thoughts which heralded perhaps but a poor production, of the labour given without return, of the bitter disappointment, and, alas ! too, of the money spent on the paper and printing which probably could be but ill spared. Taking each individual author, and regarding the agony which disappointed authorship entails, I could not but deplore the production of many a little book. Now and again the author would tell of all his trouble, and would complain of the hardness of the world which would not give him a hearing. But, looking at the thing as a whole, I know it to be good for the colonies that such efforts should be made. Success will always at last attend such struggles ; not, I fear, success for each individual struggler, but success for the people collectively, whose total of energy is thus exhibited. The desire, and the ambition, and the purpose are there, and that which a people really desires it will achieve. I cannot thus allude to the literature of the colony at large without mentioning the name of Mr. Marcus Clarke, of Melbourne, whose Australian tales are not only known familiarly by all colonists, but are almost as familiar to English readers.

Victoria has made her railways after a system,—as we are sometimes told that France did, as England certainly did not do, nor, as far as I could judge, the other Australian colonies. In the first place she has a line perfected, as far as her territory is concerned, in the direct route to Sydney. The Melbourne and Sydney road crosses the Murray at Albury, and the Victorian railway was, when I was there, nearly finished up to the Victorian side of the river, and has since been completed. I do not think that New South Wales is making any effort to fill up the gap. She has a line as far as Goulbourn,—130 miles from Sydney ; but the intervening space is so long,—about 300 miles,—that the general transit from one town to the other is still by water. The distance, and the poorness of the country to be traversed, will afford an excuse for New South Wales, the validity of which it is impossible altogether to deny; but it is, I think, notorious that Sydney is not desirous of the close intercourse which a continuous railway would create, and that she would dread the effect of the unrestricted rivalry which it would produce. The wool-growers of the intervening districts would buy in Melbourne and would sell in Melbourne, if they could reach Melbourne as easily as Sydney;—and then there would be renewed difficulty as to border duties. If all the southern part of the colony, and much of the south-eastern part, as well as the Riverina, bought their groceries in Melbourne, how would New South Wales collect sufficient taxes?

The Victorian line, striking the Murray at Albury, is a branch from a main line, previously perfected, striking the same river at Echuca, lower down. By this main route the intercourse between the Riverina and Melbourne is carried on, and from this point the people of the Riverina are anxious that a line should be made into the heart of their country, or at any rate to Deniliquin, which they call their capital. But of this they have but faint hopes while the Riverina remains a portion of New South Wales. The line from Melbourne to Echuca passes directly through the great Victorian gold-fields of which Bendigo, or Sandhurst as they now call it, is the centre. There is a station at Castlemaine, and another at Sandhurst. The line to Ballaarat, the capital of the other great Victorian gold-field,—I am afraid to call it either the first or the second in regard to its gold, but in regard to its qualities as a town there can be no doubt that it is the first,—starts from the same station at Melbourne, but branches off a mile or two from the town. This line takes an indirect course, running down the north-western side of Port Phillip Bay to Geelong, and then turning north to Ballaarat. It is intended to continue this line into the rich farming districts of the west, towards Hexham, Hamilton, and Coleraine, but when I was in the colony there was a diversity of opinion as to the route which should be taken.

There is apt to be a diversity of opinion as to the route to be taken by railways, when the money required for making them is to come from the colony at large.

Victoria, as she makes her railways, borrows the money on the credit of the entire colony, and pays the interest out of the general revenue, applying the earnings of the railways to the revenue also.   In 1869 the total interest on the amount up to that date borrowed for the construction of railways, is stated to have been £505,676, and the expenses of working the railways to have been £250,657, making a total of £756,333 expended,—whereas the proceeds earned amounted to £544,414, leaving a deficit of £211,919 to be paid out of the general taxes of the country.   I regard the result as highly satisfactory to the colony.   The railways are still in course of construction, and in that condition must be less remunerative than they will be when perfected.   I believe that comparatively a few years will make the Victorian railways self-supporting, and that an excellent discretion has been exercised in the manner in which the money has been borrowed and expended.   But it may easily be imagined that money borrowed and expended on this system should give rise to conflicting claims.   Why should one district be favoured above another, when all pay?   It will of course be urged that this district will support a railway, while that other cannot do so.   But such an argument will find no favour with the rejected district, which may perhaps be able to assert itself loudly by political support or political opposition.

Another short branch striking off from the Geelong line down to Melbourne, goes to Williamstown, which is the port of the capital, and completes the set of government railways belonging to the colony.   There is a suburban line, belonging to a private company, which runs to the south and south-east, and enables the citizens of Melbourne of all degrees to live out of the city.   It was a matter of wonder to me that a town of such a population as Melbourne should afford so very large a local traffic ;—but I soon found how large a proportion of the population lived in the suburbs which it accommodated.

There are still large districts of Victoria not touched by railway, especially the entire eastern part of the colony, which is called Gippsland, and the Wimmera district which lies to the north-west. The Gippslanders talk eagerly of a railway, but as their pleasant little capital of Sale holds only 2,000 people, and is the centre of a thinly populated country, I cannot think that their hopes will be soon gratified. The Wimmera district I did not visit. It is more remote and more sparsely populated even than Gippsland, but had I gone there, I should probably have heard of the great projected Wimmera line.

I cannot speak as highly of the coach roads as of the railways of Victoria. One effect of railways in a new country is to anticipate and supersede the creation of ordinary roads. A perfectly new country, hitherto known only to a few shepherds, is opened up by a railway,—which is not carried hither and thither for the service of towns and villages, but creates them as it goes along. Then, the one great need of a central road having been achieved, neither the government nor the inhabitants are for a time willing to go to the expense of macadamization. The badness of the roads is, however, remarkable throughout Australia,—and it is equally remarkable that though the roads are very bad, and in some places cannot be said to exist, nevertheless coaches run and goods are carried about the country. A Victorian coach, with six or perhaps seven or eight horses, in the darkness of the night, making its way through a thickly timbered forest at the rate of nine miles an hour, with the horses frequently up to their bellies in mud, with the wheels running in and out of holes four or five feet deep, is a phenomenon which I should like to have shown to some of those very neat mail-coach drivers whom I used to know at home in the old days. I am sure that no description would make any one of them believe that such feats of driving were possible. I feel that nothing short of seeing it would have made me believe it. The coaches, which are very heavy, and carry nine passengers inside, are built on an American system, and hang on immense leathern springs. The passengers inside are shaken ruthlessly, and are horribly soiled by mud

and dirt. Two sit upon the box outside, and undergo lesser
evils. By the courtesy shown to strangers in the colonies I
always got the box, and found myself fairly comfortable as
soon as I overcame the idea that I must infallibly be dashed
against the next gum-tree. I made many such journeys,
and never suffered any serious misfortune. I feel myself bound, however, to say that Victoria has not advanced
in road-making as she has in other matters.

There are three good towns in Victoria, towns which
would receive such praise on the score of architecture and
general arrangements in any country, whether new or old.
These are Melbourne, Ballaarat, and Geelong. In some
respects, a growing town with a look of growing prosperity
about it, but with still something of the roughness of the bush
in its unfinished streets, is more interesting than a full-fledged
city. There are many such in Victoria, in which the
churches, the banks, the schools, and the hotels seem to
bear a very undue proportion to the shops and private residences. And in every such a town that has had any success there is a newspaper,—or perhaps two. For a mile or
two on each side of such a town there will be made roads,
and then, by gradual but quick decrease of road-making
enterprise, the bush track will be reached. The population
is very small, 3,000 being enough to justify corporate pride
and a high position among boroughs, and even 500 sufficing
for a mayor. In all these towns rough plenty prevails. In
many of them I found that the rates of an artisan's wages
were quite as high as in Melbourne, and in some higher.
Large amounts of capital are occasionally expended on the
erection of a store, or a huge inn,—which not unfrequently
is lost to the speculator. But in a new country such losses
do not frighten other speculators ;—do not even frighten
him who for the nonce has been ruined. The man who has
lost his money " clears out," and some other speculator
comes in. I visited various such towns as these, Beechworth, Hamilton, Sale, Woods Point, Wangaratta, and others,
and was invariably struck by their uncouth prosperity. You
see them expanding and growing, as you do the young
colonial girl of ten years old, who buds forth so quickly that

the increase of her physical power becomes almost visible to
you. Too often these towns are altogether ugly to the eye.
How should an unfinished congregation of houses be otherwise than ugly when it is constructed with rectangular streets
on a level plain? The pretentious dimensions of some two
or three buildings,—of a church, a bank, or an inn,—adds
to the ugliness of the houses generally, and gives to the
stranger a feeling of mixed melancholy and of thankfulness
that his lot has not been cast in so unsightly a place. When,
however, he has learned on inquiry that every man there
earns 4*s.*, 5*s.*, or 6*s.* a day, and that meat is 2*d.* a pound,
and when he remembers that in his own pretty villages at
home men are earning 2*s.* a day and that meat is 1*s.* a
pound, the melancholy by which he is pervaded takes another
direction.

From this general charge of ugliness I must except the
pretty town of Beechworth, which is the capital of a large
district, and which is graced by a lunatic asylum. But its
charm does not depend on the greatness of its corporate
condition, or even on its asylum. It is backed by the Australian Alps, and has had bestowed upon it the gift of fine
scenery. I doubt whether there be a man alive who would
prefer 2*s.* a day and grand mountains, to 5*s.* and a flat
country ;—but when the matter does not come home so
closely to the spectators, a pretty landscape has a great
effect.

Australia makes a great deal of wine,—so much and so
cheaply that the traveller is surprised how very little of it
is used by the labouring classes. Among them some do not
drink at all, some few drink daily,—and many never drink
when at work, but indulge in horrible orgies during the few
weeks, or perhaps days, of idleness which they allow themselves. But the liquor which they swallow is almost always
spirits—and always spirits of the most abominable kind.
They pay sixpence a glass for their poison, which is served
to them in a cheating false-bottomed tumbler so contrived
as to look half-full when it contains but little. The drain is
swallowed without water, and the dose is repeated till the
man be drunk. The falseness of the glass seems to excuse

I

itself, as the less the man has the better for him ;—but the
fraud serves no one but the publican, for though the "nobbler" be small,—a dram in Australia is always a nobbler,—
there is no limit to the number of nobblers.   The concoc-
tion which is prepared for these poor fellows is, I think,
even worse than that produced by the London publican.
At home, however, beer is the wine of the country and is the
popular beverage at any rate with the workmen of this country.   In all the Australian colonies, except Tasmania, wine
is made plentifully,—and if it were the popular drink of the
country, would be made so plentifully that it could suffice
for the purpose.   All fruits thrive there, but none with such
fecundity as the grape.   One Victorian wine-grower, who
had gone into the business on a great scale, told me that if
he could get 2s. a gallon for all that he made, the business
would pay him well.   The wine of which he spoke was certainly superior both in flavour and body to the ordinary wine
drunk by Parisians.   It is wholesome and nutritious, and is
the pure juice of the grape.

Accustomed to French and Spanish wines,—or perhaps to
wines passed off upon me as such,—I did not like the Australian "fine" wines.   The best that I drank was in South
Australia, but I did not much relish them.   I thought them
to be heady, having a taste of earth, and an after-flavour
which was disagreeable.   This may have been prejudice on
my part.   It may be that the requisite skill for wine-making
has not yet been attained in the colonies.   Undoubtedly
age is still wanting to the wines, which are consumed too
quickly after the vinting.   It may possibly be the case that
though Australia can grow an unlimited quantity of wine,
she cannot produce wines capable of rivalling those of
Europe.   On these points I do not pretend to have an
opinion.   But I regard a wholesome drink for the country
as being of more importance than fine wines, even though
they should equal the produce of the vineyards of the South
of Spain or the South of France.   France and Italy are tem-
perate because they produce a wine suitable to their climate.
Australia, with a similar climate, produces wine with equal
ease, and certainly,—I speak in reference to the common

wine,—as good a quality. There is now on sale in Melbourne, at the price of, I think, threepence a glass,—the glass containing about half a pint,—the best vin-ordinaire that I ever drank. It is a white wine, made at Yering, a vineyard on the Upper Yarra, and is both wholesome and nutritive. Nevertheless, the workmen of Melbourne, when they drink, prefer to swallow the most horrible poison which the skill of man ever concocted.

CHAPTER X.

THE scheme of legislation and government is the same in Victoria as in the other colonies, but it has been carried out after a more entirely democratic fashion, and with a more settled intention of throwing the political power of the colony into the hands of the people. There are, of course, the three estates,—King, Lords, and Commons, represented here by the Governor, with his appointment from Downing Street, the Legislative Council, and the Legislative Assembly. The Governor has, of course, the royal veto; and he has also, which is much more commonly used, the power of reserving bills which have passed the two colonial houses for the approval or disapproval of the home government. The Upper House, or Legislative Council, is elective, as it is also in South Australia. In Queensland and New South Wales it is nominated. The nominations in the latter colonies are, indeed, practically made by the premier for the time, who is the minister of the people; but a House is thus constituted much less democratic and at the same time more influential than when elected by popular constituencies. Political power necessarily belongs chiefly to the Lower House,—to that which is nearest to the community at large; but it falls altogether away from an elective Upper House, as the people devote all their energies and all their thoughts to the members whom they are to elect for the popular chamber.

The Legislative Council in Victoria is returned by six provinces into which the colony is divided,—each province returning five members. Of these five one goes out every second year, so that each member of the Council is returned for ten years. A property qualification is required both for the candidate and for the electors. The former must own property to the value of £2,500, and the latter must pay a rental of £50, or rates on property to that amount. The interest taken by Victorians in the elections of the Council is not great. At those which were made in 1870 there was no contest in four out of the six provinces, and in the other two less than 50 per cent. of the electors polled. The Upper House seldom initiates laws, and is looked upon rather for protection than action. This is certainly the case in the other colonies also, but in none of them to the same extent as in Victoria. In Tasmania and South Australia I found the prime minister in the Upper House. In Queensland and New South Wales I found one of the cabinet there; and, in the latter, many of the leading men of the colony held seats in the Council. In Victoria the cabinet is no doubt represented in the Council; but the representation is generally feeble, and the gentlemen selected have of late held no office and, I believe, received no emolument.

The Lower House is elected for three years, by manhood suffrage, and no property qualification is required either for the candidates or for the electors. The votes for both Houses are of course taken by ballot. In regard to the ballot in Victoria, it is as well to point out that its value consists not in any security afforded by secrecy,—as to which the voters are happily quite indifferent;—but in the tranquillity at elections which it ensures. In Victoria, and in Victoria alone among the Australian colonies, members of parliament are paid. They receive £300 a year for their services, and are entitled to travel free by railways and mail-coaches. The system of payment has not, however, as yet been permanently adopted. Unless renewed by another bill, it will lapse after the first year of the parliament next to be elected, and would thus cease in 1875. Whether it will be renewed not a few in the colony profess to doubt; but I observe that the doubters are those who think such payment to be objectionable. I have but little faith myself in the modera-

tion of a dog that has once tasted blood, and do not therefore believe that the members of the next Victoria parliament will be endowed by so strong a spirit of patriotic
martyrdom as to abandon by their own act the salaries
which they will be then enjoying. I will not trouble my
reader here by attempting to prove that this making a pro-
fession of parliament, this power of living poorly on the
small means which parliament will produce, must be in-
jurious to the legislature of the country, as the system has
but few advocates at home. It has now been practised for
many years in the United States, and certainly has not
served there to raise the House of Representatives. It has
not been long tried in Victoria, but it certainly has not as
yet had that tendency.

The mode of carrying on the government in Victoria subject to the approval of parliament is almost identical with
that which is familiar to us at home. The governor nominally appoints his minister,—selecting one chief who selects
his own cabinet; but the choice is in fact made by the
Lower House, whose chosen leader remains in power as
long as he is the chosen one, and gives way by resignation
as soon as some other favourite has usurped the votes of the
majority. The mode of changing ministers is nearly the
same as with us at home,—but the power of the minister is
in one respect confined within narrower limits. The outgoing
minister in his last and generally futile attempt to regain
that which he has lost, recommends the Crown to dissolve
Parliament, so that the country at large may have an opportunity of reversing the last decision of its representatives.
We at home now think that the Crown is bound to follow
the advice so tendered, thereby obeying the great constitutional rule that the sovereign can do no political act except
by the advice of his ministers. The practice is not as yet
recognised,—is at any rate not as yet established as constitutional usage,—in the colonies. During my sojourn in
Australia I saw a ministry outvoted in New South Wales
and another in Victoria. In each case the outgoing minister
appealed to the governor for a dissolution. In New South
Wales the governor acceded,—and was then blamed by

every one for doing so. In Victoria the governor refused,—giving his reasons in a paper which was read to the House, and every one praised him for refusing. In the one case as in the other there was a general feeling that nothing could be gained by a dissolution,—as in New South Wales nothing was gained by the outgoing minister. Nevertheless it will come to be accepted in the colonies before long as good constitutional doctrine that in this matter, as in all other matters of political practice, the governor should be guided by his responsible advisers.

A member of a colonial cabinet is not so great a man as a cabinet minister at home. He is not even relatively so great a man, and does not hold a position among his fellow citizens proportionate to that enjoyed by our own statesmen at home ; but he holds very much more than proportionate powers, and exercises very much more than proportionate patronage. Everything is centralized. The roads, the bridges, and the railways of the colony are constructed by government. Asylums and gaols are erected and managed by the government. The lands of the colony, not as yet alienated, are the property of the government at large, and are sold or leased by the government. The local magistrates are appointed by the government. Municipal institutions are growing, and as they grow this centralization of power will be lessened; but, in the meantime, the ministers of the day, who may be men but very little qualified to bear the weight of such responsibility, are called upon to arrange details affecting the interests of individuals which it would be impossible for any minister, however great, to adjust with true impartiality. Things are, in truth, adjusted with an eye to electioneering majorities. When a member for some remote district becomes a cabinet minister, that district at once expects all the good things which patronage can give. Should a Roman Catholic be prime minister the Roman Catholics throughout the colony expect government places ; —and every porter at a railway holds a government place. But the minister for lands is he upon whom the greatest pressure is brought to bear. A supporter of the ministry considers himself entitled to buy good land cheap,—and considers also that every impediment should be thrown in the way of those who oppose the ministry but still wish to buy land. Tenders of contracts for the conveyance of mails are sent out in the name of the postmaster-general, who happened also to be prime minister when I was in Melbourne. Tenders for government clothing are sent out in the name of the treasurer. The same practice prevails throughout the cabinet, and produces a feeling that staunch support of the government may be quite as influential in procuring the desired job as favourable terms. The injustice done to individuals is not in itself so great an evil as the growing conviction throughout the colony that all this is a matter of course, and that it forms a recognised part of that concrete institution which we welcome under the name of Constitutional Government.

I do not wish to say hard things of Victorian ministers of state ;—nor do I condemn any individuals when I assert that the whole colony is permeated by a conviction that the power of government is used for jobbing. While matters are centralized as they are now,—while members of the cabinet are compelled to exercise their own judgment in the appointment of gaolers, railway porters, and letter-carriers over the entire colony,—while tenders are sent in, not to the politically powerless head of a department, but to the political minister himself by name,—it would require more than human energy and impartiality to avoid jobbery In the present circumstances of the colonial executive departments is it not probable that the energies of ministers will be prompted to take quite the other direction ? Indeed no man could sit for a month on the Victorian ministerial bench who determined to manage his office without any reference to his parliamentary position. It is taken as a matter of course that he will use his patronage for the promotion of his party.

In this matter I do not know that even yet we have our hands at home quite clean. I think I do know that they have not at any rate been long clean. But the sin has been all but abolished among us, chiefly by the intense desire of statesmen to be quit of a business that had been thrown

upon them gradually by the increasing propensity to raise
bulwarks for political powers, but which they at last found
to be not only onerous and disreputable, but also unservice-
able. In the United States the system is still rampant,---
though there it has been somewhat lessened by the general
feeling which prevails as to its iniquity. In all the Australasian colonies it exists. In each of them ministers are
driven to seek parliamentary support by manipulating
patronage. Fortunes already made are not common among
legislators in a new country,—so that it may often happen
that the brothers, sons, and kinsmen of a minister may
themselves be in need of places. A ministry that was
beaten in the parliament of Victoria in June, 1872, was
turned out solely on the ground that it had misused its
patronage. There may, perhaps, be room to hope that
such an example may be of service, and that it may tend to
teach the people generally that parliamentary government
does not mean the partial advancement of a certain class
who may support this or that set of politicians. There can
be but little doubt that a decentralization of affairs and an
increase in the power and responsibility of local management would greatly tend to save colonists themselves from
falling into a miserably false view of politics, which at
present it is almost impossible that they should avoid.

The revenue of the colony for the year ending 30th June,
1872, was £3,721,648. This included about three-quarters
of a million raised by the sale of public lands and by
pastoral leases. It included also the amount collected on
the railways, for water-supply to the city of Melbourne, for
telegraphs, pilot-dues, and postage, and various other items,
all of which are brought to the account of the public purse,
though they have no connection with the taxation of the
country The absolute burden on the country, raised in
the shape of taxes, does not exceed a million and a half,
and is therefore not above £2 a head on the population.
The public debt amounts to twelve millions,—but it has
been borrowed exclusively for the construction of public
works, and almost exclusively for the construction of railways. It must be admitted that the burden of taxation on

the public is light in the colony, and is so although the
government has undertaken enterprises on the public
behalf, which no private companies could have achieved.

The two great staple articles of commerce in Victoria are
wool and gold. Of the gold-fields of the colony I have said
enough, but it may be well to add a comparative statement
of the value of those two sources of wealth. In 1870 the
gold exported from the colony was sold for £6,119,782,
and the wool for £3,205,106. Gold maintains its nominal
value, whereas wool vacillates so much that within twelve
months the price may be nearly doubled or halved. Between March, 1871, and March, 1872, the price of wool did
rise fully 80 per cent. But since 1852, the first year of
extended gold production in Victoria, the Victorian wool
has never come near to the Victorian gold, and during the
whole of that period has amounted to little more than a
quarter of it. Nevertheless the established wealth of the
wealthy man in Victoria has been made by pastoral pursuits
rather than by mining. The aristocracy is essentially an
aristocracy of squatters,—that is of gentlemen who have
made or are making their money by grazing cattle and
shearing sheep. The gold may cost as much to raise it as
it is worth,—may, indeed, and often does, cost much more.
But the sheep increase in numbers and are shorn with comparatively little outlay. Here, as in most other countries,
land is more coveted, and seems to convey a higher influence, than any other property. The squatter, even though
he do not own his land, but runs his sheep on waste lands,
as a crown tenant with a short lease, and no certainty of
tenure even as to that, is still regarded as a territorial mag-
nate. Though the gold produced in the colony be annually
worth double the wool, and though the raids of the free-
selecter on the squatter have been more cruel in Victoria
than even in the other colonies, still the production of wool
is the most popular and certainly at the present moment the
most remunerative occupation in Victoria.

In 1870 the total imports into the colony amounted to
£12,455,758, and the exports to £12,470,014, thus very
nearly balancing themselves. Each amount is about a

million lower than it was ten years before,—in 1861. But I doubt whether this can be taken as showing any decrease in the substantial prosperity of the colony. The decrease in the exports has been chiefly on gold and live-stock, with a wholesome rise on most other articles of Victorian produce. The export of wool increased during that period by more than a third, showing that it was better worth the while of the stock-owners to keep their sheep than to send them into the other colonies for sale. The produce of gold is necessarily fluctuating, and cannot be taken in any one year as an indication of the trade of the country. The decrease in the imports was chiefly on grain and flour, thus showing that the country had progressed in the important work of feeding itself. No doubt, whenever new gold-fields are opened, creating new "rushes," or old gold-fields show themselves to be for a time specially productive, there will be a sudden influx of migratory population, and successful miners will spend money freely. They will thus raise the imports by their consumption, and the exports by the gold which they send away. A gold-producing country must be subject to these fluctuations, but they can hardly be taken as a proof either of the decay or the rise of substantial prosperity. As to the substantial prosperity of Victoria, no one, I think, who has visited that country can entertain a doubt. It is to be seen in the daily lives of the colonists, in the clothes which they wear, in the food which they eat, in the wages which they receive, in the education of their children, and in the general comfort of the people.

TASMANIA.

TASMANIA.

CHAPTER I.

EARLY HISTORY.

It seems hard to say of a colony, not yet seventy years old, that it has seen the best of its days, and that it is falling into decay, that its short period of importance in the world is already gone, and that for the future it must exist,—as many an old town and old country do exist,—not exactly on the memory of the past, but on the relics which the past has left behind it. England has towns of her own at home and colonies of her own abroad,—it would be invidious to name them,—of which this may truly be said. On visiting them the stranger feels assured that the salt of life has gone out of them. Trade dwells in them no longer, and prosperous men do not move about their streets. Their inhabitants are contented to be obscure, and generally have neither fears nor hopes. Society is mild and dull, and the remnant of the people who are left are for the most part satisfied to sit and wait. But a young colony should have young, sparkling, eager life. She should be hopeful, impetuous, and loud, with a belief in her destiny; and if she be given somewhat to boasting, she will not, indeed, thereby show herself to be possessed of an actual virtue, but will give evidence even by that vice of the strength of youth which makes a community at first buoyant and then prosperous. Such essentially are Queensland and Victoria, which force even upon unwilling ears a conviction of their strength by the loudness of their self-assertion and the vigour of their confidence. I by no means say that the dreamy, dusty quiescence of decay, the imbecility of old age which does not become actual death because so little of the energy of life is expended on the work of living from day to day, have become the lot of young Tasmania; but I do say that Tasmanians are almost united in declaring so of themselves, and that they have said so till the other colonies are quite united in repeating the story.

Tasmania as Tasmania is very young,—so young that many old-fashioned folk at home hardly recognise her under that name, and still know her as Van Diemen's Land. That name is now odious to the ears of Tasmanians, as being tainted with the sound of the gaol and harsh with the crack of the gaoler's whip; but it was under that name that the island was prosperous. England sent her convicts thither, and with her ruffians sent £350,000 a year for their custody and maintenance. The whole revenue of the island, including Customs, Inland Revenue, and Land Fund, does not now exceed £280,000. And the money sent from England was by no means all the wealth which the convicts brought with them. They had their thews and sinews, and the free squatters of Tasmania knew well how to turn such God-sends into money. And public works were done magnificently by them,—on the doing of which sufficiently, quickly, and without too close a regard to any immediate return of money, the welfare of a growing colony almost depends. Roads were made, and buildings were erected, and river-banks were cleared, and forests were cut down with a thoroughness which proved that convicts were at any rate useful. But though useful they were disgraceful. The Van Diemonians,—as colonists from other colonies are wont to call them in jeering mirth,—had a spirit of their own which could not be at ease within a prison, even though they themselves were the masters and wardens, and kept the keys of the prison. It began to be unendurable to them that their beautiful island, the sweetest in climate, the loveliest in scenery, the richest in rivers and harbours, the most accessible of all Great Britain's eastern colonies, should be known to the world only as Great Britain's gaol. So they spoke their mind, and of course had their way,—as has been the case with all Great Britain's children since the tea was thrown overboard at Boston. The convicts were made to cease, and Van Diemen's Land became Tasmania,—Tasmania with free institutions of its own, with representative government, with Lords and Commons, with a public debt, with its own taxes, and a right to govern itself by its own laws,—so long as it should enact no laws contrary to the spirit of the laws of England. It became, in fact, as were and are the other colonies, all but independent, and it threw off from itself its convict stain. But then, as a matter of course, it threw off from itself also the £350,000 a year which in one shape or another the convicts used to bring with them from England, and it could make no more roads and put up no more public buildings except in the normal way of the world, by paying the market price for the works accomplished.

The feeling of disgrace, the aspiration for a different state of things, and the determination to be quit of the questionable well-being of a convict establishment, were very grand on the part of the free settlers of Van Diemen's Land. There was more in it than in the same resolution on the part of New South Wales;—for New South Wales was large, and was achieving property in another way when it resolved that convicts should be no longer received. New South Wales made no such sacrifice as did Van Diemen's Land. The government money, and government works, and government employment were no longer at that time all in all to New South Wales, as they were to the small colony settled in the southern island, which had been created in the first place for the convicts, and then nourished by them. A great fight was made by the mother country to retain the right thus to dispose of her ruffians, and Sir William Denison, who was the governor of the day in Van Diemen's Land, was very eager in his attempt to perpetuate the arrangement, acting no doubt under instructions from the Colonial Office at home. But the feeling against the convicts was too general, and the people, though few in

K

numbers, were too strong for Sir William Denison. In 1851 and 1852, when the agitation was going on, there were less than 75,000 free inhabitants in the colony, but they prevailed ;—and as a consequence the money was stopped. There were no longer British troops in the island, now re-christened as Tasmania. All the paraphernalia of home wealth, and home empire, and home influence were withdrawn. Of course there has been a reaction. I do not dare to say that the Tasmanians regret their convicts ; but they do regret the attendant expenditure and attendant ceremonies of the convict establishment. The colony had been fostered by extraneous help and not by internal energy. It was easier to see and to feel the meanness in the eyes of the world of this position, than to rise at once to the national effort necessary for success on its withdrawal. The "Van Diemonians" were all but united in the declaration of their determination that no more convicts should be sent to them. They are now almost equally united in their declaration that the cessation of the coming of the convicts has been their ruin. They think that England has been hard to them in the measure of justice which she has meted. There might have been a regiment or at any rate a company of soldiers left in the island,—a few red jackets if only to enliven the streets and gladden the eyes of the women. Was it to be expected that all the money was to be withdrawn at once,—or if not quite at once with so great rapidity ? There still remains, and will yet remain for a few years,—as I shall explain more at length in another chapter,—a small subsidy for the expiring needs of the old establishment ; but that is becoming less and less every year, and the want of the money is felt in every station and in every shop.

We all know the listlessness and unmanly apathy which has hitherto been engendered all the world over by government pay. In England for the last twenty years we have been making great efforts to cure the evil, but the fact that the efforts have been found to be necessary is the best proof of the truth of the assertion. Government cannot get the same work out of its workmen that is got by private employers. It cannot build a ship, or manage an estate, or erect a palace with that economy which a private master can ensure. Six hours of work, diminished perhaps to five or four as opportunities may allow, takes the place of the eight hours given by servants employed in private enterprises. This scope for idleness produces idleness till it becomes the great blessing of the service that real work is not exacted. To pretend to do something,—not even to pretend to do much,—is the gentlemanlike thing. There has been much of all this in England, but more of it, I think, among Englishmen employed out of England. The evil is by no means limited to the clerk, or secretary, or commissioner who feels himself to be a great man because he has very little to do for his salary, but extends itself to all those who see and know and envy the great man. A profuse expenditure of government money in any community will taint the whole of it with the pervading sin. Men learn to regard the government as babies regard the nurse,—and are like the big calf which can only be kept from its overwrought mother's dugs by some process of disagreeable expulsion. Personal enterprise and national enterprise are equally destroyed by it. In Dublin, you are told that Dublin could not thrive if the Lord Lieutenant were withdrawn ; and, consequently, Dublin with its Lord Lieutenant does not thrive. Of all food this national mother's milk, when taken beyond the period of infancy, is the most enervating. Van Diemen's Land had the strength of character necessary for the abandonment of it by her own effort. I think myself that she has a constitution sufficiently strong to enable her to live through the consequent crisis, and to walk honestly on her own legs after a period of weakness. In the meantime she feels herself to be sick, and she longs for the unwholesome nourishment which she herself was wise enough to throw away from her.

I need hardly say that the island now called Tasmania lies south of Australia. The port of Launceston, which is the largest town in the northern division of the island, is, at the present rate of steaming, about twenty-five hours distant from the port of Melbourne. The island, with the small

adjacent islands belonging to it, is somewhat smaller than
Ireland. It comprises nearly seventeen million acres, of
which less than a fourth have been alienated from the
Crown,—that is, purchased and used by settlers in the
colony. A small portion of the vast remaining area is
leased by the Crown to squatters, and is depastured,—if I
may use a word which I have found to be common in the
colonies ; but by far the greater proportion of the island is
covered by dense unexplored forests of gum trees. It is
now divided into eighteen counties, of which five in the
west are, as far as I could learn, altogether uninhabited and
uninhabitable. Of others only strips of land near the sea
or by the side of rivers have been "taken up." It is
mountainous, the mountains boasting of but moderate altitudes,—5,000 feet, and the like. It is intersected by many
rivers, and watered by many lakes, being in this respect
altogether unlike the mainland of Australia. It was discovered in 1642, originally by Abel Jan Tasman, a Dutch-
man,—as were so many of the Australian pioneers. Tasman,
so says the legend, was violently in love with Maria, the
daughter of one Van Diemen, who in those days was
governor of the Dutch East Indian possessions. Tasman
had been sent out on this expedition by Van Diemen, and
showed his gratitude and gallantry by the liberal use of his
patron's name and that of his patron's daughter in the
nomenclature of the places he discovered. The whole
country he called Van Diemen's Land. The largest of the
adjacent islands which he saw he christened Maria. The
lady's name still stands on the maps ; but posterity, with a
justice which is not customary in such matters, after more
than two centuries, in its hatred of a sound which had become
connected all over the world with rascaldom, has gone back
to the real discoverer, and has created for the colony the
name of Tasmania. For many years after Tasman's discovery
it was thought to be a part of the continent of New Holland, as
Australia was then called. It was not till 1798 that George
Bass discovered the straits which still bear his name. In
1803 the island was first occupied on behalf of Great
Britain by a party sent from New South Wales, and in 1804

Colonel David Collins was appointed as its first lieutenant-governor, he being at that time subject to the governor of the parent colony. The settlement in Van Diemen's Land was made with the express intention of relieving New South Wales of a portion of its convicts, and specially with a view of sending thither those who had been hitherto stationed at Norfolk Island,—which place had been found to be ill fitted for the purpose. At this time the only, or at least by far the paramount, interest taken by the mother country in the possession of Australia had reference to her convicts. New South Wales had been found to be a place to which convicts could conveniently be sent ; but the number which could be safely kept there was not sufficient for the purposes of the home government. Van Diemen's Land might supply the deficiency, and to Van Diemen's Land were dispatched a certain proportion of the convicts who crowded and embarrassed the hands of the governor of New South Wales. Two stations were opened, the first on the north and the second on the south side of the island. And thus sprang up two towns, Launceston on the Tamar in the north, and Hobart Town on the Derwent in the south. These are still the chief and, perhaps I may say without offence to various flourishing villages, the only towns in Tasmania ; and they are joined together by such a road, 120 miles in length, as is not to be found elsewhere in the Australian colonies. This was, of course, made altogether by convict labour.

From this time, 1804, down to the year 1856, when responsible government began, the history of Van Diemen's Land is simply the history of a convict establishment. How to manage convicts, how to get work out of them with the least possible chance of escape, how to catch them when they did escape, how to give them liberty when they made no attempt to escape, how to punish them, and how not to punish them, how to make them understand that they were simply beasts of burden reduced to that degree by their own vileness, and how to make them understand at the same time that if under the most difficult circumstances for the exercise of virtue they would cease to be vicious, they might

cease also to be beasts of burden,—these were the tasks
which were imposed, not only upon the governors and their
satellites, not only on all officers military and civil, not only
on the army of gaolers, warders, and such like, which was
necessary, but also on every free settler and on every free
man in the island. For no one who had cast in his lot with
Van Diemen's Land could be free from the taint of the
establishment, or unconnected with the advantages which it
certainly bestowed.

A double set of horrors is told of the convict establishment of Van Diemen's Land,—of horrors arising from the
cruelty of the tyrant gaolers to their prison slaves, and of
horrors created by these slaves when they escaped and
became bushrangers. It must be borne in mind that almost
every squatter was a gaoler, and that almost every servant
was a slave. But no tidings that are told through the world
exaggerate themselves with so much ease as the tidings of
horrors. They who are most shocked at them, women who
grow pale at the hearing and almost shriek as the stories are
told them, delight to have the stories so told that they may
be justified in shrieking. The ball grows as it is rolled, and
the pile of wonder is accumulated. But no doubt the work
to be done was very nasty work, and there was of necessity
much of roughness on both sides. It must be understood
that these prisoners in Van Diemen's Land were not to be
kept as prisoners are kept in our county gaols and peni-
tentiaries at home. They were to be out at work wherever
the present need of work might be. Nor were they to be
watched when at work by regular warders as many of us
have seen to be done with gangs of prisoners at Portland,
Portsmouth, and elsewhere at home,—so watched that immediate escape, though not perhaps impossible, is very
difficult. A portion of the convicts sent to Van Diemen's
Land were no doubt locked up from the first, a portion
were employed on government works and were probably
kept under close though not continued surveillance ;—but
the majority both of men and women were sent out as
servants to the free settlers, who were responsible, if not
directly for the safe custody of those entrusted to them, at

least for immediate report should any escape. The first preliminaries of escape were easy. A man could run into the bush, and be quit at any rate of the labour of the hour. If he were shepherding sheep, or building fences, or felling timber, during the greater part of the day, no eye unless that of a brother convict was upon him. He could go, and the chances of the world were open to him. But when these first preliminaries were so easy it was of course essential that they should ordinarily be rendered unsuccessful, and that the attempt should be followed by speedy and sharp punishment. The escaped convict was at once hunted, and generally tracked by the facilities which starvation afforded to his pursuers. No one but an escaped convict would feed an escaped convict, and none but they who had established themselves as bushrangers had food either to eat or to give. Even the established bushrangers, who had homes of some sort in the mountain recesses, who were in league with the blacks, and who knew how to take the wild animals, the kangaroos and walliby and opossums, were not unfrequently driven by famine to surrender themselves.

Of course the escapes were numerous, and of course the punishments were severe. And it was not only that the men would escape, but also that when punctual to hours and punctual in the receipt of their rations, they would not earn their rations by work. They would not work after such a fashion as to please their masters ;—and, as a necessity, the masters had a redress for such occasions. A convict who would only eat rations and never earn them,—and who could not be dismissed as can an ordinary idle servant,— required some treatment more or less severe. The master himself was not allowed to inflict corporal punishment,—but the neighbouring magistrate was entrusted with that power. The magistrate could, on hearing sufficient evidence of wilful idleness or other delinquency, inflict a certain number of lashes. The thing became so common, of such everyday occurrence, that very light evidence was soon found to be sufficient. The neighbouring settler or squatter was probably the friend of the magistrate, who was a squatter himself; and what better,—indeed what other evidence could

the magistrate have than his friend's word? The practice
became very simple at last. If the man would not work, or
worked amiss, or was held to have sinned in any way against
his master's discipline, he was sent to the magistrate to be
flogged. He himself would be the bearer of some short
note. " Dear Sir,—Please give the bearer three dozen, and
return him." The man as a rule would take the note,—and
the three dozen, and would return. A bold spirit would
perhaps run away. Then he would be tracked and dogged
and starved, till he either came back or was brought back,
—and the last state of that man would be worse than the
first.

Of course these were horrors. The men who did escape,
and some who did not, committed fresh crimes and under-
went fresh trials,—with very small chance of verdicts in
their favour. And of all crimes murder and attempts to
murder seem to have been most in excess. Men were
hung for murder and attempts to murder and for various
other crimes. The hangings were frequent and gave rise to
sharp expostulations. There is a story in the island that the
gaol chaplain at Hobart Town once remonstrated,—not
against hanging in general or the number that were hung,—
but as to the inconvenient celerity with which the ceremony
was performed. Thirteen men, he said, could be comfortably hung at once, but no more. The crowding had been
too great, and he trusted that for the future the accommodation afforded by the gaol might not be too far stretched.
The hangman was a great and well-paid official. There were
flagellators also, generally convicts themselves, promoted to
the honourable employment of flogging their brethren at the
different stations. There is still, I am told, an old pen-
sioned hangman living under protection in the island. The
flagellators have disappeared, some having gone to Victoria
as miners, some having died in their bed,—a reasonable proportion having been murdered. It may be understood that
the flagellators would not be popular.

Not a few of these forlorn ones did escape and make their
way into the wilderness, living in holes and amidst rocks and
sometimes in habitations built for themselves in the deep

recesses of the forests. The names of some of these still
live in the memory of old Tasmanians, and some few still
live themselves as respectable members of society. There
was one Brady, who seems to have possessed himself of half
the mountain tops in the island, for, let the traveller go
where he will, he will be shown a " Brady's Look-out."
Brady, I think, was hung at last. And there was one Howe,
who had a wonderful career, living with a native girl whom
he at last murdered because she was not fleet enough of
foot to escape with him, and who was himself at last murdered by a companion. And then there was one Cash, who
had a long career as a bushranger, and who now lives in
dignified and easy retirement. There is also one Markham,
now carrying on business satisfactorily as a gardener, who
lived for seven years in a retreat he made for himself in the
bush, coming down occasionally and stealing such.articles as
were essential for him, growing a little wheat on a plot round
his cottage, keeping a goat and rearing a few sheep. For
seven years the man lived on in this way, all alone, undis-
covered, sufficing in all things for himself,—except in regard
to those occasional thefts from his nearest neighbour. Then
the solitude became too much for him, and he crept down
to a neighbour's house,—the squatter from whom he had
been accustomed to steal,—and finding the mistress of the
family, he gave himself up to her in order that the law might
do as it would with him. The squatter, who had been the
man's prey, was an Irish gentleman, with a tender heart,
who felt thankful to the man for not having murdered his
wife and children. Having position and influence he interfered on the man's behalf, and the law was lenient and the
man was pardoned. The story was told to me by the lady
to whom Markham surrendered himself, wild, with long
locks, clothed in a sheepskin, haggard with solitude, tired
out with absolute independence. Now he is a prosperous
grower of apples. What an episode in life for a man to
carry about always in his memory !

There was much of murder and robbery ; much of hanging
and slavery. English settlers to whom convicts were as-
signed of course learned the sweets of slavery. Their

servants were intelligent beasts of burden, who had only to be fed, coerced, and made to work. The slave too was not purchased, and if he died there was no loss. The system of course was bad, as with our present lights we can see plainly enough. But though the system was bad, the men who carried it out did, I think, mainly strive to do so to a good end. Though one hears much of flogging in Van Diemen's Land, one hears still more of the excellence of the service rendered by convicts. Ladies especially are never weary of telling how good and how faithful were the females allotted to them and to their mothers. Indeed it is from the ladies of the colony that one hears the loudest regrets in regard to the good things that have now been lost for ever. And though the ladies are the loudest, men also tell of the excellence of the convicts by whose labour they were enriched in the old days. Again, on the other hand, the inquirer is constantly startled by the respectability of career and eminent success of many a pardoned convict. Men who came out nominally for life were free and earning large incomes within comparatively few years. Unless a man were reconvicted he was sure to be made free, having at first a ticket of leave, which enabled him to work within a certain district on his own behalf, and then a conditional pardon, which allowed him to go anywhere except to England. In the records of Tasmania, which we have at home, we are told of the cruelty and sufferings inflicted and endured on both sides, of the cruelty of masters and of all that their slaves endured, of the bloodthirsty malignity of bushrangers, and of the evils which they perpetrated on the community. Horrors are always so popular that of course such tales are told the loudest. Enduring good conduct with good results creates no sensational enjoyment, and therefore we hear little or nothing of masters and mistresses so satisfied with the docility of convicts as to find them superior to free servants, or of men who have been sent from England as abject, nameless wretches, who have risen, after a period of penal service, to opulence, respectability, and almost to honour.

When the establishment was first set on foot in Van Diemen's Land, not only were convicts sent out to certain

of the settlers as labourers without hire, but the settlers who
took them had with each convict a grant of land,—so many
acres for each convict taken. The owner of the slave was
then bound to feed and clothe the man, but was not required
to pay him any wages. That the convicts were sufficiently
fed and clad by their employers I have never heard denied.
Indeed food was so cheap,—or at least meat was so,—that
no deficiency in this respect was probable. Nor, as far as I
can learn, were the men overworked. No doubt the amount
of labour performed by them daily was less than that ordinarily given by free labourers. But absolute submission was
required from them,—that absolute touch-your-hat-and-look-
humble submission which to this day is considered necessary
among soldiers. They were to give implicit obedience, and
masters accustomed to implicit obedience and absolute submission are apt to become arbitrary. And the scourge,
when it is in use, recommends itself strongly to those who
use it. The system could not but be evil. Then,—after
some years, wages of £9 per annum were required from the
masters for each man,—out of which the men found their
own clothes. This was a great improvement in the condition of the convicts, as they were thus enabled to own
property and to exercise some of the rights of free men.
At the same time they had awarded to them the privilege of
leaving their masters if they chose, and of going on to the
public works. This was a privilege which was but seldom
exercised, as private work and private rations and private
discipline were always better than the work and rations and
discipline of the public gangs. But it was something for a
man who could not endure a master to be able to shake
that master's yoke from his neck.

In different parts of the island, as the public works demanded, large stations were built for those employed. There
were various of these stations on the route from Launceston
to Hobart Town, where the men were kept while they constructed the road. They were built of stone, and the ruins
of them are still to be seen on the roadside. Here also
resided wardens and gaolers and flagellators, and I fancy
that life in the gangs was generally very much worse than

life in private service. The streets and roads about Hobart Town were made after this fashion, and many of the public buildings were put up by the convicts. The traveller is astonished at the neatness and excellence of these works in Hobart Town till he learns by degrees what it was that convict labour in old days did for a convict establishment.

And there was a third mode of bestowing the convicts in Tasmania which was,—and indeed is, for it still remains,—the most remarkable of the three. There were men who could neither be sent out as private servants, or even trusted to work in gangs,—men for whom a prison home was needed. A prison home also was needed for the new comers, as to whom in the first months of their service solitary confinement and good discipline were a part of the bad bargain they had made for themselves. This prison they were for a while established at Port Arthur, a peninsula on the other hand, the main-land by a neck of land only a few facility of career and has been, I think, in many respects the convict. Memorable, as it is probably the most picturesque, prison carrying punishment in the world. It is still in operation, as a certain proportion of old English convicts are yet in durance, and I shall therefore speak of it in the next chapter. Now it is altogether under colonial control; but it has been so only for a year or two. The transfer was, I think, finally made in 1870, till which time Port Arthur was an imperial establishment. Perhaps no spot on the globe has been the residence during the last sixty years of greater suffering or of guiltier thoughts.

The system of transportation as carried on in Van Diemen's Land no doubt was bad. It was bad to stain with the crime of so many criminals a community which must necessarily be in itself so small. It could never have been hoped that the population of Van Diemen's Land could swallow up so large a body of English criminals as would be sent thither, without becoming a people especially noted for its convict element. And yet it was never intended that Van Diemen's Land should be devoted to convicts, as was Norfolk Island, and as is the little spot of land called Spike Island in the Cove of Cork. And the portioning out of convicts to settlers to be employed as labourers was bad;

for it created a taste for slavery which has not yet lost its
relish on the palate of many Tasmanians. A certain amount
of harshness and bitter suffering was, no doubt, incidental
to it. But I do not believe that men became fiends under
its working. The fiends came out ready made, from England, and were on the whole treated with no undue severity.
Of course there were exceptions,—and the exceptions have
reached the public ear much more readily than has the true
history. Nevertheless the people rebelled against the system,
—or rather repudiated it with such strength, that the government at home was at last forced to give way.

In 1853 Van Diemen's Land ceased to receive convicts,
and in 1856, following the example of her elder and younger
sisters on the Australian continent, she went to work with
a representative government of her own. There had been
considerable difference of opinion between the colony and
the mother country. The convict establishment was very
convenient to us. We all know well how hard of solution
is the question of the future disposition of the man against
whom a judge has with great facility pronounced a sentence
of penal servitude for a certain term of years. Whither
shall we send our afflicted brother? Our depôts at home
are small and easily crowded. Van Diemen's Land in this
respect was convenient, and was at first hardly thought to
have a voice loud enough to make itself heard. The governor of the day, Sir William Denison, did what he could to
save the thing. But the people were in earnest and they
prevailed.

Up to that time the colony had no doubt prospered.
Wool, the staple of all the Australian colonies, had been
grown with great profit in the island. It was from Van
Diemen's Land that the district now called Victoria had
been first supplied with sheep. It was found that almost
every plant and almost every animal that thrives in England
could be acclimatized in an island whose climate is only a
little warmer than that of England, and a little more dry.
It became known in the East for its breed of horses, for its
whale fishery,—which was pre-eminently successful,—for its
wheat and oats, and especially for its fruit. It could supply

all Australia with fruit if only all Australia could be made to take it. For a time the markets were at any rate good enough to secure wealth. Men in Van Diemen's Land became rich, and both Launceston and Hobart Town were prosperous boroughs. Schools were general, hospitals were established, the institutions of the colony generally were excellent. Van Diemen's Land had not indeed a great reputation. It had a name that seemed to carry a taunt in men's ears. But it was prosperous and fat; and, unless when the bushrangers were in ascendency, the people were happy. Such was their history up to 1856, when transportation had been abolished and representative government was commenced. Now the Tasmanians declare themselves to be ruined, and are not slow to let a stranger know that the last new name given to the island is that of "Sleepy Hollow." When the stranger asks the reason of this ruin, he is told that all the public money has gone with the convicts, and that—the rabbits have eaten up all the grass. The rabbits, like the sheep, have been imported from Europe, and the rabbits have got ahead of the sheep. "If it was not that this is Sleepy Hollow," they say, "we should stir ourselves and get rid of the rabbits. But it is Sleepy Hollow, and so we don't."

CHAPTER II.

WHEN it had been decided between the mother country
and the colony that transportation to Van Diemen's Land
should be at an end, the colonial Houses of Parliament
petitioned the Queen that the name might be changed,—so
that the convict flavour and the convict odour attached to
the old sound might be banished ; and the Queen of course
assented. Hence has sprung in the catalogue of our colonies the name of Tasmania, as pretty as any that we have,
but to my ears somewhat fantastic. In New South Wales,
with its enormous area, and in the absence of any sea
barriers by which convicts could be hemmed in, the traveller
does not at present hear much about convicts. They have
wandered away whither they would. Now and then good-
natured reference is made, in regard to some lady or gentleman, to the fact that her or his father was " lagged," and
occasionally up in the bush a shepherd may be found who
will own to the soft impeachment of having been lagged
himself,—though always for some offence which is supposed
to have in it more of nobility than depravity. But in Tasmania the records are recent, fresh, and ever present. There
is still felt the necessity of adhering to a social rule that
no convict, whatever may have been his success, shall be
received into society. " But if he should be a member of
the Assembly?" I asked. Well, yes, my informant acknowledged that there would be a difficulty. There are occasions on which a member of the Assembly may almost
demand to be entertained,—as a member of the House of

Commons has, I imagine, almost a right to dine with the Speaker. It is not only that men and women in Tasmania do not choose to herd with convicts, but that they are on their guard lest it might be supposed that their own existence in the island might be traced back to the career of some criminal relative.

In the meantime, though a new name sweet as a rose has been invented, the odour and the flavour have not as yet quite passed away. A certain number of convicts are at work on the public domain in Hobart Town, but they are always the convicts of the island,—men who have received their sentences for deeds done in Tasmania. At the extreme south-west of the island,—in a peninsula called by the name of Tasman, which is all but an island,—is maintained a station called Port Arthur, and there are at present kept as many as remain of the old English exiles. With them are a portion of the convicts of the island. For those who were sent out from England, England still pays the cost of maintenance, amounting to £36 19s. 8d. per annum for each man under sentence, and something less for lunatics and paupers. Of these the great majority are now either paupers or lunatics, who would be free were they able to earn their own bread. England also pays, and will, by agreement, continue to pay for some further term of eight or nine years, a lump sum of £6,000 per annum towards the general police expenses, which were commenced on behalf of the mother country. When an English convict, who has had a conditional pardon, is reconvicted, he is maintained at the expense of the colony if reconvicted after a period of six months of freedom ;—but at the expense of England if within that period. And so the convict system is dying out in Tasmania, and will soon be extinct, and at last the odour and the flavour will be gone.

I visited Port Arthur, and was troubled by many reflections as to the future destiny of so remarkable a place. It is in a direct line not, I believe, above sixty miles from Hobart Town, but it can hardly be reached directly. The way to it is by water, and as there is no traffic to or from the place other than what is carried on by the government for the supply of the establishment, a sailing schooner is sufficient,—and indeed more than sufficiently expensive. In this schooner I was taken under the kind guidance of the premier and attorney-general of the island, who were called upon in the performance of their duties to inspect the place and hear complaints,—if complaints there were. We started at midnight, and as we were told at break of day that we had made only four miles down the bay, I began to fear that the expedition would be long. But the wind at last favoured us, and at about noon we were landed at Tasman's peninsula in Norfolk Bay, and there we found the commandant of the establishment and horses to carry us whither we would. We found also a breakfast at the policeman's house, of which we were very much in want.

Tasman's peninsula, which has been held entire by the Crown for the purposes of the convict establishment, is an irregularly formed piece of land about twenty-five miles long and twelve broad, indented by various bays and creeks of the sea, very hilly, covered with primeval gum-tree forest, and joined on to the island by a very narrow neck of sand. Port Arthur, where are the prisons, is about nine miles from Norfolk Bay; but our first object was to visit the neck,—called Eagle Hawk Neck,—partly for the sake of the scenery, and partly because the neck is guarded by dogs, placed there to prevent the escape of the convicts. I had heard of these dogs before I visited Tasmania, but I had thought that they were mythic. There, however, I found them, to the number of fifteen, chained up in their appointed places at and near the neck. The intention is that they should bark if any escaped prisoner should endeavour to swim at night across the narrow arm of sea which divides the two lands. In former days they used to be employed in hunting the men down. I doubt whether they are now of any service. They are allowed regular rations, one pound of meat and one pound of flour a day per dog; and I found the policemen stationed at the Neck very loud in their assurances that the business could not be carried on without the dogs. The policemen also have rations,—somewhat more than that of the dogs, though of the same kind;

L

and it struck me that to the married men who have families in the neighbourhood, the rationed dogs might be serviceable.

The scenery at this spot is very lovely, as the bright narrow sea runs up between two banks which are wooded down to the water. Then we went farther on, riding our horses where it was practicable to ride, and visited two wonders of the place,—the Blow-Hole, and Tasman's Arch. The Blow-Hole is such a passage cut out by the sea through the rocks as I have known more than one on the west coast of Ireland under the name of puffing-holes. This hole did not puff nor blow when I was there; but we were enabled by the quiescence of the sea to crawl about among the rocks, and enjoyed ourselves more than we should have done had the monster been in full play. Tasman's Arch, a mile farther on, is certainly the grandest piece of rock construction I ever saw. The sea has made its way in through the rocks, forming a large pool or hole, some fifty yards from the outer cliffs, the descent into which is perpendicular all round; and over the aperture stretches an immense natural arch, the supports or side pillars of which are perpendicular. Very few even now visit Tasman's Arch; but when the convict establishment at Port Arthur comes to an end, as come to an end I think it must, no one will ever see the place. Nevertheless it is well worth seeing, as may probably be said of many glories of the earth which are altogether hidden from human eyes.

On the following day we inspected the prisons, and poorhouse and lunatic asylum and farm attached to the prisons; —for there is a farm of well-cleared land,—seventy or eighty acres under tillage, if I remember rightly; and there is a railway for bringing down timber and firewood. The whole was in admirable order, and gave at first sight the idea of an industrial establishment conducted on excellent commercial principles. The men made their own shoes and clothes and cheeses, and fed their own pigs, and milked their own cows, and killed their own beef and mutton. There seemed to be no reason why they should not sell their surplus produce and turn in a revenue for the colony. But prisons never do turn in a revenue, and this certainly was no exception to the rule.

I found that there were altogether 506 persons, all males, to be looked after, and that no less than 97 men were employed to look after them. Of these 25 were officers, many of whom were in receipt of good salaries. There was the commandant, and the Protestant chaplain, and the Roman Catholic chaplain, and the doctor, and the doctor's assistant, and the postmaster, forming with their wives and families quite a pleasant little society, utterly beyond reach of the world, but supplied with every comfort,—unless when the wind was so bad that the government schooner could not get round to them. These gentlemen all had houses too. I was hospitably received in one, that of the commandant, which, with its pretty garden and boat-house, and outlook upon the land-locked bay of the sea, made me wish to be commandant myself. There would have been nothing peculiar in all this, except the cleanness and prettiness of the place, were it not that it must apparently all come to an end in a few years, and that the commandant's house and the other houses, and all the village, and the prisons, and the asylum, and the farm, and the church, will be left deserted, and allowed to fall into ruins. I do not know what other fate can be theirs. Tasmania will not maintain the place for her own prison purposes when there is an end of the English money;—and for other than prison purposes no one will surely go and live in that ultima Thule, lovely as are the bays of the sea, and commodious as may be the buildings.

Of the 506 men to be looked after, 284 belonged to England, and 222 to the colony. Of the 506, 234 only were efficient for work; and of this latter number only 39 were English convicts. It will be understood that the lingering English remnants of transported ruffianism would by this time consist chiefly of old men unfit for work. There were 146 English paupers,—convicts who have served their time, but who would be unable to support themselves if turned out,—and there were ten invalids who would return to their convict work when well. There were also 89 lunatics, of whom only four were still under sentence. With 506 men to be looked after, 97 officers and constables to look after them, and with only 234 men able to do a day's work, it may well be imagined that the place is not self-supporting. Its net cost is, in round numbers, £20,000; of which, in round numbers again, England pays one-half and the colony the other. It was admitted that when the English subsidy was withdrawn,—for in fact England does pay at present £6,000 a year for general expenses over and above her contribution per man to the establish-ment at Port Arthur,—that when this should be discon-tinued, Port Arthur must be deserted.

The interest of such an establishment as this of course lies very much in the personal demeanour, in the words, and appearance of the prisoners. A man who has been all his life fighting against law, who has been always controlled but never tamed by law, is interesting, though inconvenient, —as is a tiger. There were some dozen or fifteen men,— perhaps more,—whom we found inhabiting separate cells, and who were actually imprisoned. These were the heroes of the place. There was an Irishman with one eye, named Doherty, who told us that for forty-two years he had never been a free man for an hour. He had been transported for mutiny when hardly more than a boy,—for he had enlisted as a boy,—and had since that time received nearly 3,000 lashes! In appearance he was a large man and still power-ful,—well to look at in spite of his eye, lost as he told us through the misery of prison life. But he said that he was broken at last. If they would only treat him kindly, he would be as a lamb. But within the last few weeks he had escaped with three others, and had been brought back almost starved to death. The record of his prison life was frightful. He had been always escaping, always rebelling, always fighting against authority,—and always being flogged. There had been a whole life of torment such as this ; forty-two years of it ; and there he stood, speaking softly, arguing his case well, and pleading while the tears ran down his face for some kindness, for some mercy in his old age. " I have tried to escape ;—always to escape," he said,—" as a

bird does out of a cage.   Is that unnatural ;—is that a great
crime ?"   The man's first offence, that of mutiny, is not one
at which the mind revolts.   I did feel for him, and when he
spoke of himself as a caged bird, I should have liked to
take him out into the world, and have given him a month of
comfort.   He would probably, however, have knocked my
brains out on the first opportunity.   I was assured that he
was thoroughly bad, irredeemable, not to be reached by any
kindness, a beast of prey, whose hand was against every
honest man, and against whom it was necessary that
every honest man should raise his hand.   Yet he talked
so gently and so well, and argued his own case with such
winning words !   He was writing in a book when we entered
his cell, and was engaged on some speculation as to the
tonnage of vessels.   " Just scribbling, sir," he said, " to
while away the hours."

There was another man, also an Irishman, named Ahern,
whose appearance was as revolting as that of Doherty was
prepossessing.   He was there for an attempt to murder his
wife, and had been repeatedly re-tried and re-convicted.
He was making shoes when we saw him, and had latterly
become a reformed character.   But for years his life had
been absolutely the life of a caged beast,—only with inci-
dents more bestial than those of any beast.   His gaolers
seemed to have no trust in his reformation.   He, too, was a
large powerful man, and he, too, will probably remain till he
dies either in solitary confinement or under closest surveillance.   In absolute infamy he was considered to be without
a peer in the establishment.   But he talked to us quite
freely about his little accident with his wife.

There was another remarkable man in one of the solitary
cells, whose latter crime had been that of bringing abominable and false accusations against fellow-prisoners.   He
talked for awhile with us on the ordinary topics of the day
not disagreeably, expressing opinions somewhat averse to
lonely existence, and not altogether in favour of the impartiality of those who attended upon him.   But he gave us
to understand that, though he was quite willing to answer
questions in a pleasant, friendly way, it was his intention

before we left him to make a speech. It was not every day that he had such an audience as a prime minister and an attorney-general,—not to speak of a solicitor-general from another colony who was with us also, or of the commandant, or of myself. He made his speech,—and I must here declare that all the prisoners were allowed to make speeches if they pleased. He made his speech,—hitching up his parcel-yellow trousers with his left hand as he threw out his right with emphatic gesture. I have longed for such ease and such fluency when, on occasions, I have been called upon to deliver myself of words upon my legs. It was his object to show that the effort of his life had been to improve the morals of the establishment, and that the commandant had repressed him, actuated solely by a delight in wickedness. And as he made his charge he pointed to the commandant with denouncing fingers, and we all listened with the gravest attention. I was wondering whether he thought that he made any impression. I forget that man's name and his crime, but he ought to have been a republican at home, and should he ever get out from Port Arthur might still do well to stand for a borough on anti-monarchical interests.

But of all the men the most singular in his fate was another Irishman, one Barron, who lived in a little island all alone ; and of all the modes of life into which such a man might fall, surely his was the most wonderful. To the extent of the island he was no prisoner at all, but might wander whither he liked, might go to bed when he pleased, and get up when he pleased, might bathe and catch fish, or cultivate his little flower-garden,—and was in very truth monarch of all he surveyed. Twice a week his rations were brought to him, and in his disposal of them no one interfered with him. But he surveyed nothing but graves. All who died at Port Arthur, whether convicts or free, are buried there, and he has the task of burying them. He digs his graves, not fitfully and by hurried task-work, but with thoughtful precision,—having one always made for a Roman Catholic, and one for a Protestant inmate. In this regularity he was indeed acting against orders,—as there was some prejudice against these ready-made graves ; but he went on with his work, and was too valuable in his vocation to incur serious interference. We talked with him for half an hour, and found him to be a sober, thoughtful, suspicious man, quite alive to the material inconveniences of his position, but not in the least afflicted by ghostly fear or sensational tremors. He smiled when we asked whether the graves awed him,— but he shook his head when it was suggested to him that he might grow a few cabbages for his own use. He could eat nothing that grew from such soil. The flowers were very well, but a garden among graves was no garden for vegetables. He had been there for ten years, digging all the graves in absolute solitude without being ill a day. I asked him whether he was happy. No, he was not happy. He wanted to get away and work his passage to America, and begin life afresh, though he was sixty years old. He preferred digging graves and solitude in the island, to the ordinary life of Port Arthur; he desired to remain in the island as long as he was a convict; but he was of opinion that ten years of such work ought to have earned him his freedom. Why he was retained I forget. If I remember rightly, there had been no charge against him during the ten years. "You have no troubles here," I said. "I have great troubles," he replied, "when I walk about, thinking of my sins." There was no hypocrisy about him, nor did he in any way cringe to us. On the contrary, he was quiet, unobtrusive, and moody. There he is still, living among the graves,—still dreaming of some future career in life, when, at last, they who have power over him shall let him go.

Of the able-bodied men the greatest number are at work about the farm, or on the land, or cutting timber, and seem to be subject to no closer surveillance than are ordinary labourers. There is nothing to prevent their escape,— except the fact that they must starve in the bush if they do escape. There is plenty of room for them to starve in the bush even on Tasman's peninsula. Then when they have starved till they can starve no longer, they go back to the damnable torment of a solitary cell. None but spirits so indomitable as that of the man Doherty will dare to repeat the agonies of escape above once or twice.

There was a man named Fisher dying in the hospital, who had been one of those who had lately escaped with Doherty, and had, indeed, arranged the enterprise, and had gotten together the materials to form a canoe to carry them off. Before they started he had been possessed of £10, which,—so the officers said,—he had slowly amassed by selling wines and spirits which he had collected in some skin round his body, such wine and spirits having been administered to him by the doctor's orders, and having been received into the outer skin instead of taken to the comfort of the inner man. This, it was supposed, he had sold to the constables and warders, and had so realised £10. Now he was dying,—and looked, indeed, as he lay on his bed, livid, with his eyes protruding from his head, as though he could not live another day. But it was known that he still had three of the ten sovereigns about him. "Why not take them away?" I asked. "They are in his mouth, and he would swallow them if he were touched." Think of the man living,—dying, with three sovereigns in his mouth, procured in such a way, for such a purpose, over so long a term of years ;—for the man must have been long an invalid to have been able to sell for £10 the wine which he ought to have drunk ! What a picture of life ;—what a picture of death ;—the man clinging to his remnant of useless wealth in such a fashion as that !

In the evening and far on into the night the premier was engaged in listening to the complaints of convicts. Any man who had anything to say was allowed to say it into the ears of the first minister of the Crown,—but all of course said uselessly. The complaints of prisoners against their gaolers can hardly be efficacious. So our visit to Port Arthur came to an end, and we went back on the next day to Hobart Town.

The establishment itself has the appearance of a large, well-built, clean village, with various factories, breweries, and the like. There is the church, as I have said, and there are houses enough, both for gentle and simple, to take away the appearance of a prison. The lunatic asylum and that for paupers have no appearance of prisons. Indeed the penitentiary itself, where the working convicts sleep and live, and have their library and their plays and their baths, is not prison-like. There is a long street, with various little nooks and corners, as are to be found in all villages,—and in one of them the cottage in which Smith O'Brien lived as a convict. The place is alive, and the eye soon becomes used to the strange convict garments, consisting of jackets and trousers, of which one side is yellow and the other brown. If it were to be continued, I should be tempted to speak loudly in praise of the management of the establishment. But it is doomed to go, and, as such is the case, one is disposed to doubt the use of increased expenditure.

All those whom I questioned on the subject in Tasmania agreed that Port Arthur must be abandoned in a few years, and that then the remaining convicts must be removed to the neighbourhood of Hobart Town. If this be done there can hardly, I think, be any other fate for the buildings than that they shall stand till they fall. They will fall into the dust, and men will make unfrequent excursions to visit the strange ruins.

CHAPTER III.

IT is acknowledged even by all the rival colonies that of all the colonies Tasmania is the prettiest. This is no doubt true of her as a whole, though the scenery of the Hawkesbury in New South Wales is, I think, finer than anything in Tasmania. But it may be said of the small island that, go where you will, the landscape that meets the eye is pleasing, whereas the reverse of this is certainly the rule on the Australian continent. And the climate of Tasmania is by far pleasanter than that of any part of the mainland. There are, one may almost say, no musquitoes. Other pernicious animals certainly do abound, but then they abound also in England. Everything in Tasmania is more English than is England herself. She is full of English fruits, which grow certainly more plentifully and, as regards some, with greater excellence than they do in England. Tasmanian cherries beat those of Kent,—or, as I believe, of all the world,—and have become so common that it is often not worth the owner's while to pull them. Strawberries, raspberries, gooseberries, plums, and apples are in almost equal abundance. I used in early days to think a greengage the best fruit in the world ;—but latterly, at home, greengages have lost their flavour for me. I attributed this to age and an altered palate ; but in Tasmania I found the greengages as sweet as they used to be thirty years ago. And then the mulberries ! There was a lady in Hobart Town who sent us mulberries every day such as I had never eaten before, and as,—I feel sure,—I shall never eat again. Tasmania

ought to make jam for all the world, and would do so for all
the Australian world were she not prevented by certain
tariffs, to which I shall have to allude in the next chapter.
Now the Australian world is essentially a jam-consuming
world, and but for the tariffs Tasmania could afford to pick,
and would make a profit out of, the cherries and raspberries.
And this is not the only evil. The Victorians eat a great
deal of jam. No one eats more jam than a Victorian
miner,—unless it be a Victorian stock-rider. But they eat
pumpkin jam flavoured with strawberries,—and call that
strawberry jam. The effect of protection all the world over
is to force pumpkin jam, under the name of strawberry jam,
down the throats of the people.

The Tasmanians in their loyalty are almost English-mad.
The very regret which is felt for the loss of English soldiers
arises chiefly from the feeling that the uniform of the men
was especially English. There is with them all a love of
home, which word always means England,—that touches
the heart of him who comes to them from the old country.
" We do not want to be divided from you. Though we did
in sort set up for ourselves, and though we do keep our own
house, we still wish to be thought of by Great Britain as a
child that is loved. We like to have among us some signs
of your power, some emblem of your greatness. A red coat
or two in our streets would remind us that we were Englishmen in a way that would please us well. We do not wish
to be Americanised in our ways and thoughts. Well,—if
we cannot have a red-coated soldier we will at any rate have
a mail-guard with a red coat, after the old fashion, and a
mail-coachman with a red coat, and a real mail-coach." And
they have the mail-coach running through from Launceston
to Hobart Town, and from Hobart Town to Launceston,
not in the least like a Cobb's coach, as they are in the other
colonies, but built directly after that ancient and most
uncomfortable English pattern which we who are old
remember;—and they have the coachman and the guard
clothed in red,—because red has been from time immemorial
the royal livery of England.

Launceston is a clean, well-built town, and does most of

the importing and exporting business of the island. It is on the north side of the island, and therefore within easy reach from Melbourne, with which port most of the business of Tasmania is done,—exclusive of the export of wool. It has no look of decay, in spite of the evil things that are said, and at any rate appears to prosper. The scenery round Launceston is not equal to that at Hobart Town, but there are one or two very pretty walks,—noticeably those up the hill over the waterfall whence the visitor looks down upon the South Esk, which there is as pretty as the Lynn at Linton.

An English farmer hearing of land giving 60 bushels of oats to the acre, averaging over 40 lbs. the bushel, would imagine that the owner of such land ought to do well,—especially if he knew that the same crop could be raised on the land year after year. But yet land growing such crops will not give a rent, or even a profit, to the combined land-owner and farmer of 10s. an acre. The corn has to be sent into Launceston, and will not fetch when there above 2s. a bushel,—or 16s. a quarter. Now oats in England, at that weight, range I believe from 30s. to 34s. a quarter. With us the wages of rural labourers are 11s., 12s., or 14s. a week, according to the county or district. In the part of Tasmania of which I am speaking, men were receiving £30 per annum wages, with rations, consisting of 10 lbs. of meat, 10 lbs. of flour, 2 lbs. of sugar, and ¼ lb. of tea per week, worth 7s. a week. They also had cottages if married, or house-room if single,—and some extra sums of money were given to them at harvest time,—£3 or £4,—to secure their services. This altogether, would be worth 20s. or 21s. a week;—whereas living is generally cheaper to the working man in Tasmania than in England. The result is that the labourers are able to pay, and as a rule do pay, 6d. a week each for the schooling of their children. The labourer does well,—but the farmer makes but a poor profit out of his tilled land. It should be explained that on the farms which I visited,—and which belonged to a family of brothers, cousins, and uncles,—everything was done with the best implements brought out from England, and that manure was used. Hitherto the use of manure in tillage is not common in any of the colonies. It is thought to be more profitable to take what the land will give and then to leave it for awhile than to carry manure to it. Gradually, however, they who are most deeply concerned in agriculture find that there must soon be an end to a system such as this. In the district of which I am speaking wheat was subject to rust, which is the great scourge of the Australian farmer. The price of wheat in Launceston was 4*s.* 3*d.* to 4*s.* 6*d.* a bushel; but my friend told me that it would pay him better to send his wheat to London than to sell it in the colony, and that he intended to do so.

I found that ordinary day-labourers throughout the colony were getting 4*s.* a day without rations, or on an average from 9*s.* to 10*s.* a week with rations and house accommodation. The men without rations would of course be employed with less certainty of duration than those hired as permanent hands with rations. Journeymen carpenters, masons, plasterers, wheelwrights, and the like, were getting 6*s.* 6*d.* a day; domestic men-servants £30 per annum with board and lodging, and female servants about £20. I found also that all provisions were cheaper than in England, or as cheap: bacon 8*d.* a pound; butter 1*s.* to 1*s.* 6*d.*; bread 3½*d.* the 2 lb. loaf; beer, brewed in the colony and very good, 2*s.* the gallon; mutton 4*d.* a pound; beef 6*d.*; sugar 4½*d.* a pound; coffee, 1*s.* 2*d.*; tea 2*s.*; potatoes £3 a ton. I am afraid that domestic details may not be very interesting to general readers, but they may serve to afford to some intending emigrant an idea of the fate which he would meet in Tasmania.

I must say of this colony, as I have and shall say of all the others, that it is a paradise for a working man as compared with England. The working man can here always eat enough food, can always clothe and shelter himself, and can also educate his children. His diet will always comprise as much animal food as he can consume,—and if he be a sober, industrious man he will never find himself long without work. Tasmania is no doubt at present not popular with the young Tasmanian working man, because the search for gold has not hitherto been prosperous in Tasmania. The

young men go off to Victoria, though it may be doubtful
whether they improve either their comfort or their means by
the journey.   A miner in Victoria will earn from 7s. to 8s. a
day ;—the average wages were 7s. 6d. when I was at Sandhurst ; but to earn that a man must be a miner.   He must
lose time in going in quest of his work, and cannot always
readily find it.   And when he has got it, and has learned to
be a miner, and is in receipt of 45s. a week, he lives hard in
order that he may gamble in gold speculation with all that
he can save.   I think that the labourer in Tasmania has the
best of the bargain : but the desire for gold is so strong, and
the chances of fortunate speculation are so seductive, that
the young men of the island colony are gradually drawn
away.

Of males, there were in the island in 1870, in round
numbers, 27,000 under twenty years of age ;—only 10,800
between twenty and forty, and 11,500 between forty and
sixty.   These figures prove that the male population has by
far too great a proportion of old and of young for thorough
well-being and a wholesome condition.   Of females, there
were 25,000 under twenty, the number of the girls as compared with that of the boys giving one evidence among
many of the fact that the male progeny in Australia is more
numerous than the female,—a rule which applies to horses,
sheep, and cattle as well as to the human race.   Between
twenty and forty there were 12,000 women, who thus beat
the men during that, the strongest, period of life, by 1,200 ;
and between forty and sixty there were only 7,000 women,
sinking below the number of men for the same period by
4,500.   What becomes of the old women in Tasmania I
cannot say.   Between sixty and seventy there are 3,200
men, and only 1,200 women.   I cannot suppose that after
a certain time of life the Tasmanian women go to the diggings.   I am almost disposed to think that the statistical
tables of the colony show that ladies in Tasmania do not
give correct records as to their ages.   On 31st December,
1870,—and I have no information corrected up to a later
date,—there were altogether in Tasmania 53,464 males and
47,301 females,—in all 100,765.   Since 1870 the increase

has been very slight. In 1853, when transportation from
England ceased, the population was 75,000. The colony,
therefore, has not grown as have the other Australian colonies,—not as Queensland, which began her career as an
independent colony in 1859 with 18,000 inhabitants, and
had 115,000 in 1870. But even in Tasmania there has been
a steady increase, though the increase during the last few
years has been small.

The road from Launceston to Hobart Town is as good
as any road in England, and is in appearance exactly like
an English road. It was made throughout by convicts, and
was manifestly made with the intention of being as like an
English road as possible. The makers of it have perfectly
succeeded. When it passes through forest land,—or bush,—
the English traveller would imagine that there was a fox
covert on each side of him. There are hedges too, and the
fields are small. And there are hills on all sides, very like
the Irish hills in county Cork. Indeed it is Ireland rather
than England to which Tasmania may be compared. And,
as I have said before, English,—or Irish,—coaches run
upon the road ; a night mail-coach, with driver and guard
in red coats, and a day coach with all appurtenances after
the old fashion. I found their pace when travelling to be
about nine miles an hour. We went by the mail-coach as
far as Campbelltown,—a place with about 1,600 inhabitants,
which returns a member to parliament, and has a municipal
council, four or five resident clergymen, a hospital, an agricultural association, and a cricket-club. Quite a place !—
as the Americans say. When I asked whether it was prosperous, my local friend shook his head. It ought to be the
centre of a flourishing pastoral district. It is the centre of a
pastoral district, which is not flourishing,—because of the
rabbits. This wicked little prolific brute, introduced from
England only a few years ago, has so spread himself about,
that hardly a blade of grass is left for the sheep ! But why
not exterminate him, or at least keep him down ? I asked
the question with thorough confidence that the energies of
man need not succumb to the energies of rabbits. I was
told that the matter had gone too far, and that the rabbit

had established his dominion. I cannot, however, but imagine that the rabbit could be conquered if Tasmania would really put her shoulder to the wheel.

We passed a place called Melton, at which a pack of hounds was formerly kept,—so called after the hunting metropolis in Leicestershire; and as I looked around I thought that I saw a country well adapted for running a drag. Foxes, if there were foxes, would all be away into the mountains. They used to hunt stags, but I should have thought that the stags would have taken to the hills. But the hunting had belonged to the good old prosperous convict days, and had passed away with other Tasmanian glories. At Bridgewater, within ten miles of Hobart Town, there is a magnificent causeway over the Derwent, about a mile long, which was of course built by convict labour, and which never would,—in Tasmania never could—have been made without it.

Hobart Town, the capital of the colony, has about 20,000 inhabitants, and is as pleasant a town of the size as any that I know. Nature has done for it very much indeed, and money has done much also. It is beautifully situated,—as regards the water,—placed just at the point where the river becomes sea. It has quays and wharves, at which vessels of small tonnage can lie, in the very heart of the town. Vessels of any tonnage can lie a mile out from its streets. It is surrounded by hills and mountains, from which views can be had which would make the fortune of any district in Europe. Mount Wellington, nearly 5,000 feet high, is just enough of a mountain to give excitement to ladies and gentlemen in middle life. Mount Nelson is less lofty, but perhaps gives the finer prospect of the two. And the air of Hobart Town is perfect air. I was there in February,—the height of summer,—having chosen to go to Tasmania at that time to avoid the great heat of the continent. I found the summer weather of Hobart Town to be delicious. And there were no musquitoes there. I have said something about Australian musquitoes before. They were not so bad as I had expected; but in certain places they had been troublesome,—especially at Melbourne. But I knew nothing

of them in Hobart Town.   Other living plagues there were
plenty in Tasmania,—no doubt introduced, as were the
rabbits, with the view of maintaining the general likeness to
England.   All fruits which are not tropical grow at Hobart
Town and in the neighbourhood to perfection.   Its cherries
and mulberries are the finest I ever saw.   Its strawberries,
raspberries, apples, and pears are at any rate equal to the
best that England produces.   Grapes ripen in the open air.
Tasmania ought to make jam for all the world, and would
make jam for all the Australian world, were it not for Australian tariffs.   Tasmanian jams would probably come to
England if Tasmania could import Queensland sugar free
of duty.   As it is, fruit is so plentiful that in many cases it
cannot be picked from the trees.   It will not pay to pick it!
   So much in regard to the gifts bestowed by nature upon
the capital of Tasmania.   Art,—art in the hands of convicts,—has made it a pretty, clean, well-constructed town,
with good streets and handsome buildings.   The Government House is, I believe, acknowledged to be the best
belonging to any British colony.   It stands about a mile
from the town, on ground sloping down to the Derwent,—
which is here an arm of the sea, and lacks nothing necessary for a perfect English residence.   The public offices,
town-hall, and law courts are all excellent.   The supreme
court, as one of the judges took care to tell me, is larger
than our Court of Queen's Bench at Westminster.   The
Houses of Parliament are appropriate and comfortable with
every necessary appliance.   They are not pretentious, nor
can I say that the building devoted to them is handsome.
There is a Protestant bishop of course, and a cathedral,—
which a stranger, not informed on the subject, would mistake for an old-fashioned English church in a third or fourth
rate town.   I was told that it is tumbling down ; but a very
pretty edifice is being erected close by its side.   The work
is still unfinished and funds are needed.   Perhaps a generous
reader might send a trifle.
   From Hobart Town various expeditions may be made
which amply repay the labour.   I have already told how I
went to Port Arthur.   I was very anxious to get to Lake

M

St. Clair, but did not succeed. Lake St. Clair is nearly in the middle of the island,—somewhat towards the west, or wilder part of it,—in County Lincoln, and is, I was informed, wonderfully wild and beautiful. It was described to me as another Killarney, but without roads. The beauty, too, I was told, could be well seen only from a boat, and there was no boat then on the lake. I found that I could not compass it without devoting more time than I had to spare, —and I did not see Lake St. Clair. I went up the Derwent to New Norfolk and Fenton Forest, and across from Hobart Town to the Huon River and a township called Franklin, finding the scenery everywhere to be lovely. The fern-tree valleys on the road to the Huon are specially so,— and in one of these I was shown the biggest tree I ever saw. I took down the dimensions, and of course lost the note. It was quite hollow, and six or seven people could have sat round a table and dined within it. It was a gum-tree, bigger I imagine in girth, though not so tall as that which I described as having been found in Victoria, near the road from Woods Point to Melbourne. The River Huon is a dark, black, broad stream, running under hanging bushes,— very silent and clear, putting me in mind of the river in Evangeline.

On the Upper Derwent, in the neighbourhood of New Norfolk, where the river Plenty joins the Derwent, there are the so-called Salmon Ponds. Now these salmon ponds are a matter of intense interest in Tasmania, and very much skill and true energy have been expended,—and no slight amount of money also,—in efforts to introduce our river fish, especially the trout and salmon, into Tasmanian waters. In reference to trout the success has been perfect. The quantity in the rivers is already sufficient to justify the letting of fishing licenses at 20s. a year, and men who know how to fly-fish can get excellent sport. I have seen trout six and seven pound weight, and have eaten I think better trout in Tasmania than ever I did in England. In regard to salmon I can only say that there has as yet been no success. No one has as yet caught a Tasmanian salmon, though there are stories about of salmon having been seen. The man who catches the first salmon will be entitled to £30 reward.*

Mr. Allport, of Hobart Town, a gentleman who has taken pains with the subject, and who thoroughly understands it, is confident of success. He gave me reasons to show how it is that the salmon should take much longer than the trout to establish themselves, and to prove that there was as yet no reason for a faint heart on this great matter. Mr. Allport's enthusiasm was catching, and I found myself ready to swear, after hearing him, that there must be salmon. Some other great scientific authority has declared,—thinks I believe that he has proved,—that it is impossible that there should be a salmon in Tasmania. It is a great question. I myself, in my ignorance, lean to Mr. Allport's side altogether, because I had the advantage of knowing Mr. Allport. I was only told of the adverse great authority. But the trout are a fact. I ate them again and again, with great satisfaction. I do not doubt that before long, with true Australian fecundity, they will swarm in Tasmanian rivers.

In this part of the Island,—the part of which New Norfolk is the centre, about twenty-four miles up the Derwent from Hobart Town,—hops have lately been introduced with success. They grow with great luxuriance, and bear heavily. It is, indeed, hard to find anything that will not flourish in Tasmania,—except wheat, which seems in the Australian colonies generally to be of all crops the most hazardous. Everywhere one hears of rust. The stalk becomes hard, red, and thick under the influence of the sun, and then the grain is either not produced at all, or is a withered, shrivelled atom, giving no flour. Respecting the hops, I asked whether that at any rate was not a profitable enterprise. It would be, I was told, but for the damnable Victorian tariffs which had been invented with the primary object of ruining Tasmania,—of bringing her so low that, to escape absolute ruin, she should be forced to annex herself to her big and cruel sister. That is the Tasmanian creed, and it is one not altogether unfounded on facts. It must be understood that

* Since these words were first published the first salmon has, I am informed, been caught, and the reward given.

Victoria is the natural market for Tasmanian produce. Set-
ting wool aside, which almost as a matter of course goes to
England, and which constitutes above a third of the total
exports from the colony, we find that nearly three-fourths of
its surplus produce is shipped for Victoria. This is done in
the teeth of the terrible Victorian tariffs, and we may therefore be sure that the proportion would be much greater, and
the produce sent very much more extensive, if the Victorian
markets were open. Permission to sell her produce in Melbourne is the one thing necessary to ensure prosperity to Tasmania. This refers to almost everything she produces,—to
flour, wheat, oats, barley, fruit, jam, vegetables, cheese, butter,
hides, and horses. I always take delight in reminding a Victorian,—who is a jam-loving creature,—that he is obliged to
eat pumpkin jam, a filthy mixture just flavoured with fruit,
because of the tariff by which he protects the fruit-grower of
Victoria,—who after all can't grow fruit. I know that this
will bring down wrath on my head, because fruit is grown in
Victoria,—very fine fruit, which I have seen and eaten. And
how shall I be believed when with the same breath I warm
my fingers and cool them;—when in the same paragraph I
declare that the fruit is grown and is not grown? Money
and care no doubt will produce fruit in Victoria;—but even
Victorian shearers and Victorian miners cannot afford to eat
jam made from costly fruits. Over in Tasmania fruit is
rotting,—fruit as fine as any that the world can produce,—
because it is thought expedient to protect the Victorian
raspberry. Oh, my Victorian friend, deluging your unfortunate inwards with pumpkin trash, it grieves me to think
that the madness of this protection will not make itself
apparent to you, till your taste will have been polluted and
your digestion gone! You will, I fear, never live to learn
what comforts, what luxuries, what ample bounties the rich
world will give to him who will go out freely and buy what
he wants in the cheap markets;—or how great, how fiendish,
how unnatural is the injury done by him who won't let
others go out and buy! In the meanwhile Tasmania sits
pining because she cannot sell her fruit,—cannot sell her
hops.

Wool is at present the staple of this colony,—as of all the others. But pastoral interests do not prosper here as they do in the four great colonies on the continent. Although comparatively so small a portion of the land has been bought from the Crown,—less than four million out of a total of nearly seventeen million acres,—very few flocks are pastured on runs leased from the Crown. There are altogether in Tasmania 1,350,000 sheep; and of these all but about 100,000 are pastured on purchased lands. In 1870 the sum derived by the colony from leases was only £7,210. In 1853 it amounted to very nearly £30,000. No doubt this has been caused by the sale of lands which had before been let ; but the fact shows that it has not been found expedient to take up new lands for pastoral purposes, nor is it worth the wool-grower's while to do so. By far the greatest portion of the island is unfit even for pastoral purposes,—is too rough, too inaccessible, too rocky, and too heavily timbered. The grasses used for wool are not there,—or if there cannot be reached.

I must not misuse the colony by omitting to say a word of her gold-fields. She has gold-fields,—especially that at Fingal. I believe I shall hardly be wrong in saying that there is no other to which it is necessary to call special attention. But even on the Fingal gold-digging, very much has not yet been done. The young men of Tasmania who run to gold-rushes seek their fortunes beyond the island. Nevertheless, gold that pays has been found in the north-eastern part of the colony, and it may be that even yet Tasmanian rushes will come into fashion.

The form of government in Tasmania is very much the same as in the other colonies. There is a " Legislative Council " or Upper House, and an " Assembly," which is the Lower House. The governor of course is king, and is politically irresponsible. The Council is elected, and goes out by rotation, each man sitting for six years. The Assembly is elected for three years. In the latter manhood suffrage is the rule,—it being necessary that a man should be twenty-one years old, and have resided for a certain number of months in his district. For the Legislative Council there is a property qualification. Votes are of course taken by ballot. The chambers were not sitting when I was in Tasmania, and I was informed that they do not sit on an average above two months in the year. Legislation in the colony is undemonstrative and unexciting. But I think that a quiet common sense prevails which makes it unnecessary that a Tasmanian should blush when he compares the legislative doings in his parliament with the work of any other colony.

It strikes an Englishman with surprise to find repeated in so small a community as that of Tasmania all the fashions of government with which he has been familiar at home, but which, while he has acknowledged them to be good and serviceable for their required purposes, he has felt to be complex and almost confused,—and which he has known to have been reached not by concerted plan, but by happy accident, or rather by that arranging of circumstances which circumstances effect for themselves, when the intentions of men in regard to them are honest and high-minded. When a ministry at home is in a minority on any important subject,—any subject as to which the ministry has pledged itself,—the ministers resign in a body, and the Queen, at the advice of the outgoing premier, sends for that premier's chief political enemy. If that enemy, on assuming power, finds that the majority which brought him there will not support him while he is there, he—goes to the country. A new House of Commons is elected, and as that House may have a bias this way or that, this or that political chieftain becomes the Queen's adviser. The system is complex, and very difficult to be understood by foreigners. Even Americans find it difficult of comprehension. We call it constitutional, but it is written nowhere. There is no law compelling the beaten minister to resign. There is no law compelling the monarch to send for a perhaps unpalatable politician. There is no standard by which the importance of measures can be measured,—so that a man may say, On this measure a beaten minister will retire; but in regard to that measure a ministry, though beaten, may hold its ground. But by those who attend to politics at home the working of

the thing is understood, and the system has become constitutional. No minister could live who would put himself
into direct opposition to it, let his genius and statesmanship
be what they might. Nor could any sovereign oppose it,
and continue to be a sovereign in England. The system is
supported by no law, but by a general feeling which is
stronger than all laws,—and that general feeling of what is
expedient makes, and builds up, and alters from time to
time the political arrangement of public matters which
we call our constitution. We understand, not accurately
indeed, but after some fashion, this slow growth, and gradually self-arranging political machinery among ourselves at
home who are an old people. But it is very singular that
the same system should have been adopted with com-
placency,—almost without thought,—by our democratic
children. The Australian colonies claim to govern themselves in everything, to make what laws they please, to have
what public ministers they choose, to spend what money
they think right,—to be bound to the mother country only
by their loyalty to the Crown. They do choose their own
ministers, and give them what name they like. In one
colony they have a colonial secretary, in another a chief
secretary. In one colony it is reckoned that this secretary
must be, and in another that he only may be, the head of
the government. One colony delights to call its minister
the premier, another taboos the name altogether. One
colony has seven cabinet ministers, another six, another
five. Tasmania has only four, one of whom has neither
portfolio nor salary. In these matters they independently
make their own arrangements. But the system under which
ministers go out and come in, dissolve parliament, and live
upon majorities,—under which the governor is advised by
the retiring chieftain to send for the then popular rising
star,—even though he, the governor, should think the then
popular rising star to be the most inefficient and dangerous
man in the colony,—is the exact copy of our political constitutional system at home.

The revenue in Tasmania amounts to about £220,000 a
year, and the expenditure has been a little higher. I do

not give the exact sum, because the figures before me will be an old story before this is published. The public debt amounts to £1,328,000, which includes a sum of £400,000 advanced to the Launceston and Deloraine Railway. The taxation only just exceeds £2 a head, and cannot therefore be regarded as heavy. There is a separate land fund, which is burdened with expenses incident to the land. The amounts received for sale and leases of crown lands are expended on the land or on public works, so that no abso-lute revenue is thus received.

CHAPTER IV.

THAT Tasmania is going gradually to the mischief seems to be the fixed opinion of Tasmanian politicians generally. That such a belief as to one's country should not be accompanied by any personal act evincing despair, has been the case in all national panics. English country gentlemen have very often been sure of England's ruin ; but I have never heard of the country gentleman who, in consequence of his belief, sold his estate and went to live elsewhere. Speculative creeds either in politics or religion seldom prove their sincerity by altered conduct. Modern prophets have more than once or twice named some quick-coming date on which the world would end ; but the prophets have made their investments and taken their leases seemingly in anticipation of a long course of future years. So it is in Tasmania. Even they who are most unhappy as to the state of things live on comfortably amidst the approaching ruin. What the stranger sees of life in the island is very comfortable. The houses are well built, and are kept in good order. The public offices are clean, spacious, and commodious. The public garden is large, and, for so small a place, well kept and handsome. The inns are fairly good, as also are the shops. I here speak both of Hobart Town and Launceston, the only two towns in the colony. Hobart Town in round numbers has 20,000 inhabitants, and Launceston 11,000. But they have the appearance of large and thriving cities much more than have towns with a similar population in England. Nevertheless, the Tasmanians acknowledge it to be the fact that Tasmania is going to the mischief.

The loudest grumblers declare that the ruin is to be found rifest in the rural districts, among the country folk and poor people. Hobart Town, they say, is kept alive by visitors who flock to it for the summer months from the other colonies ; and Launceston has whatever relics of prosperous trade the island still possesses. The people in the rural districts, they say, are generally so poor that they can with difficulty live. I have, however, already stated how infinitely superior is the condition of the Tasmanian labourer to that of his brother at home in England.

No doubt, however, there are grounds for grumbling ; or it might be more just to say that there is cause for apprehension. Though Tasmania is as yet only seventy years old, as a country inhabited by white men, and, being still in its early youth, it should be yearly laying up new blood and new bone in the shape of increased population. It is not doing so. For some years past there has been no increase of which the colony can boast. During four years, from 1866 to 1870, the total increase was 403. As 340 emigrants, chiefly German, were brought into the colony in 1870 by a system of bounties,—a number so small as to show that the effort was a failure,—it must be acknowledged that those immediate attractions which give increased population to a young colony have departed from it. And the grumblers are justified also by the condition of trade generally. In 1861 the eight chief articles exported from Tasmania were as follows :—

Wool	Value £326,000
Wheat	82,000
Oats	81,000
Sperm oil	59,000
Timber	55,000
Fruit (including jams)	50,000
Horses	42,000
Flour	39,000
	£734,000

In 1870 the amounts were altered as follows :—

Wool	. . . .	£246,000
Wheat	. . . .	15,000
Oats	. . . .	56,000
Sperm oil	. . . .	33,000
Timber	. . . .	37,000
Fruit (including jams)	. . . . .	84,000
Horses	. . . .	5,000
Flour	. . . .	11,000
		£487,000

These figures show a decrease in every article except fruit; a total decrease of £247,000,—or, in round numbers, about one-third,—and a decrease of £120,000 in corn and flour alone. No doubt for so small a community such a falling off is very serious, and justifies apprehensions. Such a diminution in the supply of wheat would lead to the fear that the colony would soon fail to feed itself with flour and grain, did not we know that the exportation of these articles from Tasmania had been stopped by the Victorian tariffs. As long as Victoria charges 9d. a hundredweight on the importation of all grain, Tasmania will be shut out from the market which is nearest to her,—indeed, from the only foreign market to which she has hitherto been able to sell her produce other than wool.

In regard to wool, which is still the staple of the colony, and as to which the above figures show the greatest decrease, the circumstances admit of a certain amount of explanation. The weight of the wool exported in 1870 was as great as that produced in 1861,—indeed, something greater; and the fall in the figures is due to the depreciation in value,—which, as all persons interested in the Australian colonies are aware, has again risen very greatly since the crop of 1870 was sold. And, again, the time of shearing, which varies according to circumstances of the year, threw over a portion of the wool of 1870 to the sales of 1871. It appears that in 1868 the amount of Tasmanian wool sold was 6,136,426 lbs.; in 1869, 5,607,083 lbs.; and in 1870, only 4,146,913 lbs. The great difference apparent between 1868 and 1870 was caused by the later shearing of the latter year, and therefore does not show, as it might seem to do, any serious decay in the pastoral interest of the colony.

In respect to the other articles enumerated,—especially in regard to cereal produce,—there is evidence of decay where especially there should be increasing life; and it is of extreme importance that they who are interested not only in this colony, but in the Australian colonies generally, should inquire and understand how it has come to pass that in a land so gifted as Tasmania,—in a land more fitted by climate for English emigrants than, I believe, any other on the face of the earth,—in a land that might flow with milk and honey, in a country possessing harbours, rivers, and roads,— things should already be going from bad to worse, instead of from good to better. The convict system no doubt brought with it much of evil for which it must answer,—as also many advantages with which it should be credited. The profuse expenditure of government money, and the use of what may be called slave labour, no doubt had a tendency to paralyze the energies of the settlers. The condition produced was unwholesome, and such unwholesomeness clings long. But the Tasmanians themselves understood this, and got rid of the thing. The convict flavour is quickly passing away from them; and though a certain lack of vitality among some classes may still be due to the condition of a convict settlement as I have endeavoured to describe it, Tasmania will gradually throw off that disease as New South Wales has already done. But there are other diseases which she cannot throw off,—or rather there is another cause for disease of which she cannot rid herself,—as long as the existing unnatural position of the Australasian colonies towards each other in regard to commerce remains unaltered. I will state here the populations of the colonies roughly :—

Victoria has						750,000 souls.
New South Wales						500,000 ,,
South Australia						185,000 ,,
Queensland						120,000 ,,
Tasmania						100,000 ,,

| Western Australia | . . . | 25,000 souls. |
| New Zealand | | 250,000 ,, |

Putting aside New Zealand,—which, however, is quite as much interested in the matter as the others,—we find that they are like so many English counties, or, as the area is very large, like so many American states, contiguous to each other, speaking the same language, having the same or similar interests, connected in and out by joint properties, joint families, and joint names, attached to the same mother country, having nothing but a name to mark their borders. There is indeed no such dissimilarity of interests as between Lancashire and Wiltshire, for wool is the staple produce of each of them. There is no such cause of disruption as between the Southern and Northern States of America,— no dissimilarity of character as between the Eastern and Western States. They are at least as much one people as are the inhabitants of the dominion of Canada. They are much more one people than were the various German nationalities who had found it to be impossible not to bind themselves together by a customs union, even before Prussia had bound them together politically. They are all English;—and not a law can be passed by them without the assent of an English minister or his deputy. And yet they levy customs duties among each other as do the various nations of Europe;—or rather as did the various nations of Europe before the principle of free-trade had been efficacious in liberating a single branch of commerce.

It is not my purpose here to discuss free trade, or to attempt to prove its beneficent action. I am content in my humble way to point out that people who reject free trade must be content to eat pumpkin mixture and call it strawberry jam. Those of my readers who are still in favour of protecting home industry by duties on imported goods will not be converted by me. In regard to the great majority of my countrymen I may take it for granted that on this matter we are of one opinion. The question here is not one of free trade;—but of free trade between the Australian colonies, which may be accompanied by any amount of protection by them all against the outside world.

It is as though we should have discussed the expediency of border customs between Lancashire and Yorkshire at a time in which we levied duties on silks from France and Italy. There was a question among us then,—a much-vexed question,—as to the imposition of duties on foreign articles; but no man would have been listened to for a moment who would have proposed border customs between our counties at home. Such a man would have been simply insane. The man who should do so in America with regard to the different states would be equally so. The German Zollverein showed what was the feeling of Germany generally in the matter. But the Australian colonies still act against each other as though they were separate nations.

And they are forbidden by the English law as it at present stands to do otherwise,—though the English government has more than once offered to the colonies its sanction for the abolition of the absurdity in the gross. As the law stands at present any British colony, and therefore any one of the Australias, may levy what taxes and what customs duties it thinks fit to levy; but it cannot levy differential duties. New South Wales for instance may put what duty it shall please on sugar;—but it cannot receive Queensland sugar free of duty and charge a duty on sugar from the Mauritius or from Cuba. And yet there is no more than a nominal border-line between the two colonies, the two places being as closely joined as any two English counties. Victoria may receive wheat free from all the world; but she cannot receive wheat free from South Australia, with which she borders as Yorkshire does with Lancashire, unless she receive it free also from all the world. The law has been so fixed in order that no dependency of Great Britain should be able to sin against that free-trade policy by which England professes to regulate her dealings with foreign countries. Differential duties may, no doubt, be levied with the express view of injuring the trade of an especial country; and if England binds herself not to commit the injury, it is intelligible that she should bind her dependent colonies to the same extent.

But England has in point of fact abandoned the principle

in regard to intercolonial trade ;—not because it is felt that
the principle is not as applicable to the colonies as to England, but on the conviction that Australia in regard to trade
must and should be regarded as one whole,—as is the
Canadian dominion, as are the United States, as were the
German kingdoms when Germany was politically divided.
A reference to the population of the colonies, to their
geographical position and affinities, to their joint interests,
to their real oneness as a people, convinces the merest tyro
in political economy of the absurdity of border duties between them,—almost equally of the absurdity of duties levied
from port to port. On the 15th July, 1870, the Secretary
of State for the Colonies wrote the following circular to the
different Australian governors :—

" SIR,—I think it important to ensure that the governors of the
Australian colonies should not misunderstand the views of Her Majesty's
government with regard to intercolonial free trade.

" The different colonies of Australia are at present, in respect of
their customs duties, in the position of separate and independent
countries. So long as they remain in that relation, a law which
authorised the importation of goods from one colony to another on
any other terms than those applicable to the imports from any foreign
country would be open, in the view of Her Majesty's government, to
the objection of principle which attaches to differential duties.

" But Her Majesty's government would not object to the establishment of a complete customs union between the Australian colonies,
whether embracing two or more contiguous colonies, or,—which would
be preferable,—the whole Australian continent with its adjacent islands.
If any negotiations should be set on foot with this object you are at
liberty to give them your cordial support.

(Signed) " KIMBERLEY."

I cannot think that any one will read this without agreeing with Lord Kimberley, though probably most who do so
would express their agreement in stronger terms, as to the
present condition of Australian customs duties than it would
suit a Secretary of State to use. But this proposition on
the part of Lord Kimberley altogether abandons the question as to differential duties between the colonies. If there
were an Australian customs union New South Wales would
get Queensland sugar free of duty, but might still charge
what duty it pleased on Cuban sugar. Victoria would

import free wine from New South Wales,—which she does largely,—and free wine from South Australia, and free hops from Tasmania ; but would still put what duties she pleased on French wines, and Chilian wheat, and English hops. And this permission would be given, not because English statesmen have gone back in their opinion about differential duties,—but because the maintenance of hostile trade interests between communities so bound together as are these colonies is a worse evil than the semblance of differential duties which would thus be allowed to exist.

But the colonies are not ready for a customs union. Three of them, Tasmania, South Australia, and New Zealand, have expressed a general concurrence ;—others a qualified concurrence. Victoria is the greatest sinner in the matter,— being for the time wedded to protection in all its deformity. In the meantime permission has been asked by certain of the colonies,—and notably by Tasmania, on whose behalf the matter has been argued with great vigour by her minister, Mr. Wilson,—that they should be allowed to arrange their intercolonial customs without reference to the duties charged on extra-colonial articles,—and that they should be permitted to do this, as a measure paving the way to a customs union. This permission has been refused them, and I must acknowledge that in the correspondence which has taken place on the subject I think that the Tasmanian statesman gets the better of Downing Street. I give in an Appendix, No. 3,— as they are too long for insertion in the text,—Lord Kimberley's circular dispatch on the subject, dated 13th July, 1871 ; and Mr. Wilson's memorandum in answer to it.

We cannot prevent the colonists from entertaining protectionist principles,—cannot go back to a condition of things which would enable the mother country to dictate to the colonies on the subject. Universal suffrage undoubtedly assists protection. The fabricator of any article sees that a tax on that article when imported will force the world around him to use the article home-made, and that then his peculiar labour will be fostered and protected. If foreign boots be made dear by a tax, the local bootmaker can get 5s. a pair for making boots ; but if foreign boots be sold cheap, he cannot get above 3s. 6d. The Victorian farmer,—a very small man usually,—thinks that he cannot grow wheat and live if wheat from Adelaide be admitted to the markets on the same terms as his own wheat. Men learn so much quickly. The lesson is acquired on the first aspect of the matter. The consequent evil results to these shallow pupils in having to pay double for goods which they consume and do not produce, requires a deeper insight into matters, and an insight accompanied by some calculation, before it produces a conviction. At home, in England, the working man is certainly not superior in intelligence to his Australian brother, but he is subjected in his political instincts and inquiries to higher and, I must say, to more honest influences. I cannot bring myself to believe that he is generally made to understand great political truths, but he is made to believe that this or that politician is a safe political guide, and he votes accordingly. And on one subject, which is to him of all the most important,—the subject of food,—he has been made to understand that free trade means a cheap loaf. In Australia food is plentiful, and the labourer feels comparatively little solicitude on this subject. Each man wishes to protect from competition that which he himself makes. The Victorian, in his wisdom, desires to give nothing out of his store to any fellow-labourer from South Australia or from Tasmania ;—at any rate to give as little as possible. He therefore is a protectionist :—and the would-be minister of the day is a protectionist because he wants the labourer's vote.

It is thus that protection has become rife, and we cannot cure the evil suddenly by any order to be given, or by any permission to be refused. The ordinary educated traveller in the colonies,—getting into the society which will fall naturally in his way,—will find that almost every person he meets is opposed to protection. But everybody will tell him at the same time that protection cannot be abolished. The voters like it, and the voters are omnipotent. There is a variation in the feeling in the various colonies ;—but this is the general state of the colonial mind on the subject. If it be so, it should, I think, be the object of governments at

N

home to develop as far as possible all operations which will
tend in the first place to create intercolonial free trade.
The existing state of things has the double evil,—the first
natural evil of impeding trade and of impoverishing everybody concerned; and the further evil of fostering rivalries
and hostilities between people who are in fact one and the
same. That a general customs union would, of all steps in
the right direction, be the greatest and the wisest there can
hardly be a doubt. To me it seems to be almost equally
clear that any measure tending to abolish customs duties
between the colonies would be a step towards a customs
union. Let New South Wales be enabled to take free sugar
from Queensland, and Queensland will take fruit on the
same terms from New South Wales. The condition of the
colonies makes it obvious that there should be no customs
levied between them.

Poor little Tasmania is straining every nerve to obtain the
privilege of sending her produce for the consumption of her
sister colonies, especially of Victoria, without which privilege
she cannot continue to exist. The value of the exports
from any country are, or should be, but small in comparison
with the value of the produce consumed at home;—but the
smaller the country is, the more certain is the ruin entailed
upon it by prohibition from selling its goods in an outside
market.

Its condition becomes such as that would be of a small
wheat-growing English county debarred from selling its
wheat beyond its own confines. The richness of its own
produce would become its own greatest burden. Industry
and energy would naturally disappear. A large population
with diverse employments, producing all, or nearly all, that
it wants, can live in such a condition, though the life would
be a bad life;—but a small community would be as were
Robinson Crusoe and his man Friday, wanting almost all
that man requires, though overladen with much plenty.

There is a remedy at hand for the injury which Tasmania
now suffers,—but it is a remedy which she cannot adopt
without soreness of heart, without dishonour, without self-
annihilation. She can become a part of Victoria, and then

the Victorian markets will be open to her. Let her implore Victoria to take her, and then she will be able to sell her wheat and her oats, her fruit and her jam, her hops and her horses at Melbourne. "You had better do it," the Victorian says to the Tasmanian. "It will come at last."

Men in Tasmania are beginning to feel that perhaps they had better do it, though the idea is odious to them. It is impossible that this island ever should be amalgamated with the big continental colony on equal terms. Were the arrangement made on seemingly equitable terms, on terms fixed in accordance with the population, Tasmania would send to the Victorian legislature one Tasmanian for every eight Victorians,—or thereabouts; and the men so sent would have to remain in Melbourne for eight or nine months of parliamentary work. This small minority would be almost voiceless among their louder brethren, and it would soon come to pass that Tasmanians would not go there. Tasmania would be represented by Victorians, to whom she would have to pay the salaries which Victorian legislators now receive. Hobart Town would no longer be a seat of government. Some judge would come there on periodical visits as often as Victorian generosity would permit, and that judge would be Victorian. The little colony would be handed over, bound hand and foot, to her strong-fisted sister, and there would be the end of all her glories. The reader will perhaps feel that these are simply sentimental objections, and will say that the material advantages to be gained would more than compensate them. But sentimental grievances are of all grievances the heaviest to bear, and the material advantages are only those which the colony has a right to expect without any sacrifice of her honour.

Such a change of things would be detrimental not only to Tasmania, but to all Australia generally. I have suggested in a former paragraph that a general federal union of these colonies into one nationality will take place sooner or later. Such I believe to be the opinion of almost all who have thought upon the subject. But nothing will tend so much to delay this result as the special greatness and superiority in population and wealth of any one colony. The

big colony will think twice before it will admit the little
colony to equal terms with it.   There was much generosity
on foot when Virginia and New York united themselves
with Rhode Island, and a great patriotic idea was urgent in
the breasts of great patriots.   Among the Australian colonies
each colony recognises with astonishing accuracy its own
position in wealth and population.   Victoria is even now
much the biggest.   Were Tasmania to become a part of
Victoria, I fear that the difficulty of forming, first, a customs
union and then a political federal union, would become
greater even than it is at present.

It is to be presumed that such amalgamation could not
be effected without the consent of the government at home,
and that the matter is one as to which a Secretary of State
would feel himself justified in refusing his consent on the
ground of general policy.   If there is to be an Australian as
well as a Canadian dominion, or rather a union of states,—
for such must be the condition rather than the other,—it
will be more easily effected with many than with a few.
Before that day shall arrive, there will probably be a
northern colony in Queensland, and a further division from
New South Wales in the direction of the big rivers.   And
there will be a northern territory in that which is all now
called South Australia, with a capital at Port Darwin.   I
trust that the fairest and prettiest and pleasantest of all the
colonies will not then have been absorbed, so that the name
of Tasmania shall be absent from the roll of Australian
States.

APPENDIX.

APPENDIX No. I., page 87.

Regulations under which free-selections of Land can be made in Victoria, taken from MacPhaile's Australian Squatting Directory.

For Crown lands, not being lands included in any city, town, or borough, licenses to occupy for a period of three years, at a rental of 2*s.* per acre per annum, any such license not to be for more than 320 acres, may be granted by the Governor to any person applying and paying half a year's rent in advance for such allotment.

Applications for licenses may be made on any day during office hours, personally, to a land officer for the district, and applicants shall at the time of application deposit half a year's rent of allotment in advance. Every license shall be issued under the following conditions :—(1.) A condition for the payment of the fee in advance at half-yearly intervals. (2.) A condition that the licensee will not, during the currency of such license, assign the license, nor transfer his right, title, and interest therein, or in the allotment therein described, or any part thereof, nor sublet the said allotment or any part thereof, and that the license shall become absolutely void on assignment of such license, whether by operation of law or otherwise, or upon the said allotment or any part thereof being sublet. (3.) A condition that the licensee shall, within two years from the issue of such license, enclose the land described in such license with a good and substantial fence, and shall, during the currency of such license, cultivate at least one acre out of every ten acres thereof. (4.) A condition annulling the license in case of non-payment of the fees, or any of them, in accordance with the conditions herein mentioned, or in case the licensee shall not, within six months after the issue of the license, and thenceforward during the continuance of such license, occupy the allotment, or in case substantial and permanent improvements certified in writing under the seal of the Board or under the hands of arbitrators to be of the value of £1 for every acre and fractional part of an acre of the allotment shall not have been made on the allotment, by the licensee, his executors, or administrators, before the end of the third year from the commencement of the license, or in case of the breach or non-fulfilment of any of the conditions of the license, or of a violation of any of the provisions of this Act. (5.) A condition that if the licensee shall, during the said period, occupy the allotment for not less than two years and a half, and shall fence and cultivate as herein provided, and make the improvements of the nature and value in the previous condition mentioned, on the allotment during the said period of three years, and shall prove to the satisfaction of the Board (to be certified under its seal) by such evidence as the Board may require that he has complied with the said conditions, and with all other conditions of the said license, he shall be entitled at any time, within thirty days after three years from the commencement of the license, to demand and obtain from the Governor a Crown grant, upon payment of 14s. for each acre or fractional part of an acre, or otherwise he may obtain a lease of the said allotment; and every such lease shall be for a term of seven years, at a yearly rent payable in equal parts half-yearly in advance of 2s. for each acre or fractional part of an acre so demised, and shall contain the usual covenant for the payment of rent, and a condition for re-entry on non-payment thereof; and upon the payment of the last sum due on account of the rent so reserved, or at any time during the term, upon payment of the difference between the amount of rent actually paid and the entire sum of £1 for each acre, the lessee, or his representatives, shall be entitled to a grant in fee of the lands leased, and every such grant shall be subject to such covenants, conditions, exceptions, and reservations as the Governor may direct : Provided that in the case of the death of the licensee during the currency of such license it shall not be obligatory on the executors or administrators of such licensee to comply with the said condition of occupation.

No such license or lease shall give power to any licensee, lessee, or assignee to search for or to take any metal; and it is provided that before any license or lease is issued to any applicant, he shall make a declaration on oath before a justice, in a form settled by the regulations, that his application is made in conformity with the provisions of this Act.

No person shall become the licensee, either in his own name or in the name of any other person, of any allotment, who shall have selected, under any previous Land Act, the maximum number of 320 acres allowed under this Act, or who shall have taken up a pre-emptive right, or shall have made a selection, or whose selection shall have been forfeited or cancelled for the evasion of any such Act. But a selecter under any previous Act may take up a sufficient quantity of land to make up the 320 acres allowed by this Act.

No person shall become the licensee of any allotment who is under eighteen years of age, or who is a married woman not having obtained a decree of judicial separation, or who is a trustee, servant, or agent in respect of the license applied for, or who has entered into any arrangement to permit any other person to acquire, by purchase or otherwise, the allotment or any part of it, or the applicant's interest in the usufruct of it, and all land applied for under this Act shall be so applied for *bonâ fide* for the use and benefit of the applicant in his own proper person, and not as the agent, servant, or trustee of any other person, on pain of the forfeiture of the license, and all contracts made in violation of the Act shall be held to be illegal and absolutely void both at law and equity.

If it be proved to the satisfaction of the Board within sixty days of the end of the third year from the commencement of the license that substantial and permanent improvements of the value of £1 per acre of the allotment have been made upon it, in the terms of the condition of the license, a certificate under the seal of the Board, to that effect, shall be given to the licensee, his executors or administrators. But if the Board be not satisfied that such improvements of the value aforesaid have been made, then such improvements as have been made may be valued by arbitration, one arbitrator being chosen by the licensee, his executors or administrators, another by the Board, and a third by the two arbitrators so chosen ; and such arbitrators, or any two of them, shall make their valuation in writing within four months after the end of the third year from the commencement of the license. But if either party shall neglect to appoint an arbitrator, then the one chosen by the other party shall have full power to value.

The Board shall, as soon as possible after the last days of June and December in every year, prepare a list of the names of all persons from whom fees or rent shall have become due on leases granted under the Land Act, 1862, or the Amending Land Act, 1865, on leases or licenses under this part of this Act, and who shall not have paid such fees or rent, and the days upon which such fees or rent become due, and such list shall be forthwith published in the "Government Gazette," and the insertion in such list of the name of any person from whom such fees or rent have become due, shall be *primâ facie* evidence of the non-payment of such fees or rent, and shall be evidence of notice to the parties named that their fees or rent are due, and that payment thereof has been lawfully demanded.

The licensee, the lessee, and assigns of an allotment of land shall have all the rights against trespassers which at law belong to the owner in possession of any land, except the right of impounding; but so soon as the allotment, or the part of it trespassed on, shall have been properly fenced, then they shall have that right also.

Holders of licenses of land under any other Act, of which the licensees shall have been in possession at least two years and a half, if it be proved to the satisfaction of the Board that they have erected buildings or other improvements on such lands, and that the conditions of the license have been complied with, and there be no objections on account of the ground being auriferous, or other reasons of a public nature, shall have the exclusive right to purchase the allotment on which such improvements stand, at a price to be determined by the Board not to exceed the upset price of the nearest land sold by the Crown before the issue of such license, and so much of the rent paid by the licensee during his possession of the land shall be credited to him in the purchase money of the said land.

Appendix No. II., page 72.

Melbourne Botanic Garden, 21st *February,* 1872.

TO CLEMENT HODGKINSON, ESQ., ASSISTANT-COMMISSIONER OF
LANDS AND SURVEY.

Sir,—Referring to your suggestions of the 12th inst., I took the
earliest opportunity of acting upon them, and accordingly, on the 15th
inst., I proceeded to the Watts River, and carefully inspected the
heavily timbered country extending from Mount Monda to Mount
Juliet, also the various spurs and tributaries of the Watts, extending as
high up as the crest of the dividing range and the watershed of the
Goulbourn River.

I have now the honour to report that a very large extent of the above
country is densely timbered with various species of Eucalypti, consisting
principally of Eucalyptus obliqua, E. Amygdalina, and E. Goniocalyx.

Immense numbers of each of the above species have attained gigantic
dimensions, and very much surpass any other species of Eucalypti I
have ever met with in other forests.

On penetrating into many of the secluded spots near the source of the
Watts, and on the spurs of the ranges in the vicinity, I met with large
tracts of valuable timber; enough to supply all ordinary demands for
many years, if carefully conserved. In many places I observed large
areas where the axe of the splitter is yet unknown, and where the
timber averages from 100 to 150 trees per acre, with a diameter of from
2 ft. to 6 ft., and from 250 ft. to 300 ft. in height, the most of which is
as straight as an arrow, with very few branches.

Some places, where the trees are fewer and at a lower altitude, the
timber is much larger in diameter, averaging from 6 ft. to 10 ft., and
frequently trees of 15 ft. in diameter are met with on alluvial flats near
the river. These trees average about ten per acre; their size, sometimes, is enormous. Many of the trees that have fallen through decay
and by bush fires measure 350 ft. in length, and with girth in proportion. In one instance I measured with the tape line one huge specimen
that lay prostrate across a tributary of the Watts, and found it to be
435 ft. from its roots to the top of the trunk. At 5 ft. from the ground
it measures 18 ft. in diameter, and at the extreme end where it has
broken in its fall, it is 3 ft. in diameter. This tree has been much burnt
by fire, and I fully believe that before it fell it must have been more
than 500 ft. high. As it now lies it forms a complete bridge across a
deep ravine.

Proceeding from Fernshaw up the Black Spur, some large specimens
of Eucalyptus obliqua and Amygdalina may be seen; but it is only by
leaving the main road and following some of the splitters' tracks for
several miles higher up the Watts that the forests of fine timber and
large trees are to be found. On some spurs of these ranges, where the

timber is extra fine in quality, some few trees have been felled by splitters, but the mountainous nature of the country, and the difficulty of transport, is so great, it will be many years before much destruction can be done in this part of the forest.

The number of splitters at present working in these forests is very limited, and is likely to continue so. In many places they have to carry their paling and shingles for long distances on pack-horses. The ranges are so steep that it is a work of much difficulty to convey them to some accessible spot. However, the splitter in this region seldom meets with a hollow tree, and he takes care to select such trees only as will turn out from 10,000 to 20,000 palings, and frequently a much greater number.

The only destruction at present to be dreaded in these forests is fire. The scrub is so dense that it is difficult to penetrate far into it, and frequently fire is used to clear a track, and in its progress makes sad havoc.

Many of the deep ravines and sides of creeks in this locality abound with splendid specimens of native beech (Fungus Cunninghamii), some of which measure upwards of 100 ft. high, with a diameter of trunk from 5 to 8 ft. This timber is of great value, and ought to be strictly preserved. Great quantities of blackwood (Acacia Melanoxylon), of large dimensions and fine quality, are everywhere interspersed throughout these forests, mixed with sassafras trees (Atherosperma Moschatum) and dogwood (Pomaderris apetala), also of large size. Lomatia Fraserii also forms a goodly sized tree in the fern-tree gullies, along with Acacia decurrens, many of which have attained the height of 150 ft., with magnificent straight trunks of from two to three feet in diameter. The timber of this species is well adapted for staves for wine casks and other purposes.

Seeing that such large quantities of valuable timber abound in the valley of the Watts, and on the spurs adjacent, I would respectfully beg to recommend the reservation of every acre, wherever it would not interfere with settlement, for, as a whole, the timber in the locality of the Watts, and ranges adjacent, is of far more value than the land, and it is rare to find such forests of sound timber in any other part of Victoria.

I have the honour to be, Sir, your most obedient servant,

WILLIAM FERGUSON, Inspector of State Forests.

Appendix No. III., page 176.

CORRESPONDENCE AS TO THE CREATION OF A CUSTOMS UNION AMONG THE COLONIES.

CIRCULAR.

Downing Street, 13*th July*, 1871.

SIR,

I HAVE had for some time under my consideration Despatches from the Governors of several of the Australasian Colonies, intimating the desire of the Colonial Governments that any two or more of those Colonies should be permitted to conclude agreements securing to each other reciprocal Tariff advantages; and reserved Bills to this effect have already reached me from New Zealand and Tasmania.

It appears that whilst it is at present impossible to form a general Customs Union, owing to the conflicting views of the different Colonial Governments as to Customs Duties, the opinion extensively prevails, which was expressed at the Intercolonial Conference held at Melbourne last year, in favour of such a relaxation of the Law as would allow each Colony of the Australasian Group to admit any of the products or manufactures of the other Australasian Colonies Duty free, or on more favourable terms than similar products and manufactures of other Countries.

At the same time it has not been stated to me from any quarter that the subject urgently presses for the immediate decision or action of Her Majesty's Government; and I trust, therefore, that any delay that may arise in dealing with it will be attributed to its true cause, namely, to the desire of Her Majesty's Government to consider the subject deliberately in all its bearings with a view to arrive at such a settlement as may not merely meet temporary objects, but constitute a permanent system resting upon sound principles of commercial policy.

The necessary consultations with the Board of Trade and with the Law Officers have unavoidably been protracted to a late period of the Session; and if Her Majesty's Government were satisfied that they could properly consent to the removal of the restrictions against Differential Duties, it would not be possible now to obtain for so important a measure the attention which it should receive from Parliament. It is by no means improbable that the introduction of a Bill to enable the Australasian Colonies to impose Differential Duties might raise serious discussions and opposition both in Parliament and in the Country, on the ground that such a measure would be inconsistent with the principles of Free Trade, and prejudicial to the commercial and political relations between the different parts of the Empire ; and I feel confident that the Colonial Governments will not regret to have an opportunity afforded them of further friendly discussion of the whole subject, after learning the views of Her Majesty's Government upon it, before any final conclusion is arrived at. I will therefore proceed to notice those points which seem to Her Majesty's Government to require particular examination.

The Government of New Zealand appears from the Bill laid before the House of Representatives, and from the financial statement of the Treasurer, to have originally contemplated the granting of special bonuses to goods imported into New Zealand from the other Australasian Colonies. As, however, this expedient was not eventually adopted, I am relieved from the necessity of discussing the objections to such a mode of avoiding the rule against Differential Duties.

The proposal now before me raises the following questions; viz.,—

1. Whether a precedent exists in the case of the British North American Colonies for the relaxation of the rule or law now in force.

2. Whether Her Majesty's Treaty obligations with any Foreign Powers interfere with such relaxation.

3. Whether a general power should be given to the Australasian Governments to make reciprocal Tariff arrangements, imposing Differential Duties, without the consent of the Imperial Government in each particular case.

4. Whether on grounds of general Imperial policy the proposal can properly be adopted.

The Attorney-General of New Zealand, in his Report accompanying the reserved Bill, observes that its main provisions are almost a literal copy of provisions which have been for some time past in force in Canada and other North American Colonies; and I observe that in the various communications before me the argument is repeatedly pressed that the Australasian Colonies are entitled to the same treatment in this respect as the North American Colonies. It may be as well, therefore, to explain what these provisions actually are.

I enclose extracts from the Acts of Newfoundland and Prince Edward Island of the year 1856; but I need not dwell upon them, because, as dealing with a limited list of raw materials and produce not imported to those Colonies from Europe, they are hardly, if at all, applicable to the present case; and I shall refer only to the Act passed by the Dominion of Canada in 1867 (31 Vict. cap. 7), which is the enactment principally relied upon as a precedent.

Schedule D of this Act exempts from Duty certain specified raw materials and produce of the British North American Provinces; and the 3rd Section enacts, that "any other articles than those mentioned in Schedule D, being of the growth and produce of the British North American Provinces, may be specially exempted from Customs Duty by order of the Governor in Council."

This, which was one of the first Acts of the Legislature of the newly constituted Dominion in its opening Session, was passed in the expectation that, at no distant date, the other Possessions of Her Majesty in North America would become part of the Dominion; and the assent of Her Majesty's Government to a measure passed in circumstances so peculiar and exceptional cannot form a precedent of universal and necessary application,—although I am not prepared to deny that the

Australasian Governments are justified in citing it as an example of the admission of the principle of Differential Duties.

With reference to the second question, as to the existence of any Treaty the obligations of which might be inconsistent with compliance by Her Majesty with the present proposal, the Board of Trade have informed me that this point could only be raised in connection with the terms of the Treaty between this Country and the Zollverein of 1865, extended through the operation of the "most favoured nation" Article to all other countries possessing rights conferred by that stipulation.

The 7th Article of that Treaty, which extends the provisions of previous Articles to the Colonies and Foreign Possessions of Her Majesty, contains the following provision :—

"In the Colonies and Possessions the produce of the States of the Zollverein shall not be subject to any higher or other Import Duties than the produce of the United Kingdom of Great Britain and Ireland or of any other Country of the like kind." I am advised that this 7th Article may be held not to preclude Her Majesty from "permitting the Legislature of a British Possession to impose on articles being the produce of the States of the Zollverein any higher or other Import Duties than those which are levied on articles of the like kind which are the produce of another British Possession, provided such Duties are not higher or other than the Duties imposed on articles of the like kind being the produce of the United Kingdom of Great Britain and Ireland."

But, apart from the strict interpretation of the Treaty, it seems very doubtful whether it would be a wise course on the part of the Australasian Colonies, which both as regards Emigration and Trade have more extensive relations with Germany than with perhaps any other Foreign Country, to place German products and manufactures under disadvantages in the Colonial markets.

Proceeding to the third question, whether, if the principle of allowing the imposition of Differential Duties were conceded, the Colonies could be permitted to impose such Duties without the express sanction of the Imperial Government in each particular case, you will be prepared, by what I have already said, to learn that I consider it open to serious doubt whether such absolute freedom of action could be safely given.

Her Majesty's Government are alone responsible for the due observance of Treaty arrangements between Foreign Countries and the whole Empire : and it would be scarcely possible for the Colonial Governments to foresee the extent to which the trade of other parts of the Empire might be affected by special Tariff agreements between particular Colonies.

It must, moreover, be anticipated that these differential agreements, being avowedly for the supposed benefit of certain classes of the community, would be liable to be affected by temporary political circumstances. The door having been once opened, each producing or manufacturing interest, and even individuals desirous of promoting any new enterprise, might in turn press for exceptionably favourable treatment under the form of Intercolonial reciprocity, while the real grounds for such changes as might be proposed would be intelligible only to those concerned with local politics.

It would appear, therefore, to be by no means clear that Her Majesty's Government could be relieved from the obligation of examining the particulars of each contemplated agreement, however limited; and while it would be very difficult for them to make such an examination in a satisfactory manner, a detailed inquiry of this kind could hardly fail to be irksome to the Colonies, and to lead to misunderstandings.

It remains for me, lastly, to ask how far it is expedient, in the interests of each Colony concerned, and of the Empire collectively, that the Imperial Parliament should be invited to legislate in a direction contrary to the established commercial policy of this country.

Her Majesty's Government are bound to say that the measure proposed by the Colonial Government seems to them inconsistent with those principles of Free Trade which they believe to be alone permanently conducive to commercial prosperity; nor, as far as they are aware, has any attempt been made to show that any great practical benefit is expected to be derived from reciprocal Tariff arrangements between the Australasian Colonies.

At all events I do not find anywhere among the papers which have reached me those strong representations and illustrations of the utility or necessity of the measure which I think might fairly be expected to be adduced as weighing against its undeniable inconveniences.

It is, indeed, stated in an Address before me that the prohibition of differential Customs treatment "operates to the serious prejudice of the various producing interests of the Australian Colonies." I understand this and similar expressions to mean that it is desired to give a special stimulus or premium to the Colonial producers and manufacturers, and to afford them the same advantage in a neighbouring Colony over the producers and manufacturers of all other parts of the Empire and of Foreign Countries as they would have within their own Colony under a system of Protective Duties. What is termed reciprocity is thus in reality protection.

It is, of course, unnecessary for me to observe that, whilst Her Majesty's Government feel bound to take every proper opportunity of urging upon the Colonies, as well as upon Foreign Governments, the great advantages which they believe to accrue to every country which adopts a policy of Free Trade, they have relinquished all interference with the imposition by a Colonial Legislature of equal duties upon goods from all places, although those duties may really have the effect of protection to the native producer.

But a proposition that in one part of the Empire commercial privileges should be granted to the inhabitants of certain other parts of the Empire to the exclusion and prejudice of the rest of Her Majesty's subjects, is an altogether different question; and I would earnestly request your Government to consider what effect it may have upon the relations between the Colonies and this country.

Her Majesty's subjects throughout the Empire, and nowhere more than in Australasia, have manifested on various occasions of late their strong desire that the connection between the Colonies and this Country should be maintained and strengthened; but it can hardly be doubted that the imposition of Differential Duties upon British produce and manufactures must have a tendency to weaken that connection, and to impair the friendly feeling on both sides, which I am confident your Government, as much as Her Majesty's Government, desire to preserve.

I have thought it right to state frankly and unreservedly the views of Her Majesty's Government on this subject, in order that the Colonial Government may be thoroughly aware of the nature and gravity of the points which have to be decided; but I do not wish to be understood to indicate that Her Majesty's Government have, in the present state of their information, come to any absolute conclusion on the questions which I have discussed.

The objections which I have pointed out to giving to the Colonies a general power of making reciprocal arrangements would not apply to a Customs Union with an uniform Tariff; and although such a general union of all the Colonies is, it appears, impracticable, it may be worth while to consider whether the difficulty might not be met by a Customs Union between two or more Colonies.

I have the honour to be,
Sir,
Your most obedient humble servant,
KIMBERLEY.

Governor Du Cane.

TASMANIA.

MEMORANDUM.

LORD KIMBERLEY's Despatch, under date of the 13th July, 1871, on the question of Intercolonial Reciprocity, has received the attentive consideration of His Excellency's Advisers.

It is satisfactory to find that the Secretary of State admits that, in the cases of Newfoundland and Prince Edward Island in 1856, and of the Dominion of Canada in 1867, Her Majesty's Government have assented to Acts exempting Colonial products from the duties imposed on similar articles when imported from Europe: and that, as regards the latest precedent, Lord Kimberley is "not prepared to deny that the Australasian Governments are justified in citing it as an example of the admission of the principle of Differential Duties."

It is not easy to understand why the earlier precedents are not similarly recognised as applicable to the recent demand for an admission of the same principle by the Legislatures of New Zealand and Tasmania, to which may now be added that of South Australia. The lists of articles in the sections of Statutes appended to the Despatch comprise, in the main, the products and manufactures of the Provinces and Colonies therein named. And the Reciprocity Conventions contemplated by the reserved Bills of Tasmania and New Zealand would deal similarly with the products and manufactures of the Australasian Colonies.

There is, however, another example of the admission of the principle of Differential Duties by Her Majesty's Government which is not referred to by Lord Kimberley. The Acts of the Legislatures of Victoria and New South Wales which sanction the reciprocal importation across the Murray Border of goods, which are liable to Customs Duties on the wharves of Melbourne and Sydney, have received Her Majesty's assent, and constitute a recent and conspicuous precedent for legislation in favour of Intercolonial Reciprocity: and this example derives special importance from the fact that the Acts in question were passed in the exercise of powers to legislate on this point, specially conferred upon Victoria and New South Wales by the Imperial Statutes which granted to those Colonies their present Constitutions.

It would, therefore, seem that all the precedents that can be instanced of Imperial assent to Colonial Legislation on this point may be " cited as examples of the admission of the principle of Differential Duties."

When we come to the extent to which such Colonial Legislation would affect Her Majesty's Treaty obligations with Foreign Powers, it is admitted that there is but one Treaty in existence which contains a stipulation restricting the fiscal legislation of " Colonies and Possessions" of the British Crown; and that the Secretary of State is "advised " that the Article in question " may be held not to preclude Her Majesty from permitting "—to quote the language of the Dispatch —" such a relaxation of the Laws as would allow each Colony of the Australasian Group to admit any of the products or manufactures of the other Australian Colonies duty free, or on more favourable terms than similar products and manufactures of other countries."

From this we may infer that, while Her Majesty is bound to require that Differential Duties shall not be imposed upon imports into British Colonies from the United Kingdom and Foreign States, Her Majesty is not required by any Treaty to refuse the Royal Assent to Measures admitting the reciprocal importation between two or more British Possessions, duty free, of articles which the Colonial Legislatures have subjected to Customs Duties when imported from Europe.

Lord Kimberley's suggestion of the impolicy of placing " German products and manufactures under disadvantages in the Colonial markets," seems to touch a subject on which it may be said the Legislatures of Australasia are the legitimate, perhaps the best, judges.

Lord Kimberley's observations on the question of Colonial Differential Duties as affecting the general Imperial Policy seem to proceed upon a misconception of the object aimed at by the Australasian Governments, and of the motives which influence the advocates of the removal of Imperial restrictions on the fiscal legislation of the Colonies.

The object of the Tariff Conference held in Melbourne last year was to establish a Commercial Union of the Australias and New Zealand on the basis of a common Tariff, with a distribution of the Customs Revenue to the several Colonies according to population. That object was found to be, at that time, unattainable; and the Conference adopted a unanimous Resolution to the effect that it was desirable that the Colonial Legislatures should be freed from Imperial restrictions on their reciprocal fiscal arrangements.

Her Majesty's Government had intimated their readiness to assent to a Customs Union of two or more Colonies; but, when such an arrangement was found to be impracticable, the Governments represented at the Conference were willing to rest content with the removal of the existing restrictions on Intercolonial trade by Reciprocity Conventions.

It is difficult to apprehend the force of objections offered to this mode of treating the question when no objection is raised to a Customs Union, which would produce precisely analogous results on a much larger scale.

A Customs Union between all the Australasian Colonies would enable these Countries to impose, if it were thought desirable, protective duties upon imports from Europe, while Colonial products and manufactures were reciprocally interchanged duty free. How, it may be asked, can such a system be deemed legitimate and admissible, when a plan for carrying it into only partial operation by less direct means is held to be open to grave objections?

Her Majesty's Government are prepared, we are informed, to sanction an arrangement that would enable a group of six Colonies, if they were so minded, to establish absolute Free Trade among themselves in combination with Protection against all the world beside. But when two Colonies desire to be placed in a similar position by a Tariff Convention, "Her Majesty's Government are bound to say that the measure proposed seems to them inconsistent with those principles of Free Trade which they believe to be alone permanently conducive to commercial prosperity."

By Lord Kimberley's own showing there are precedents for the legislation now submitted for the Royal assent; and there are no legal obstacles to its recognition in the shape of Imperial Treaty obligations. It is only on an abstract theory of the superior advantages of a Free Trade policy that the Secretary of State objects to a proposal which seems to sanction Protection under the name of Reciprocity.

These are views which can find no acceptance with Colonial Legislatures under a system of Constitutional Government. The question they desire to solve is one directly affecting the interests of the communities for which those Legislatures are elected to make Laws. Its effect upon Imperial interests is almost inappreciable. The doubt whether "the imposition of Differential Duties upon British produce and manufactures might not have a tendency to weaken the connection between the Mother Country and the Colonies, and to impair the friendly feeling on both sides," seems scarcely warranted by a fair consideration of the whole bearing of the application under discussion.

It may be observed that the Tariffs of the Australasian Colonies have, in effect, for some years past imposed duties on British manufactures either intentionally or incidentally protective.

Is it to be supposed that the "friendly feeling on both sides" which has survived the imposition of Protective or Prohibitory Duties on

British manufactures would be "impaired" by a Reciprocity Convention,—for example, between Victoria and Tasmania,—which permitted the products and manufactures of those Colonies to be mutually exchanged duty free, or under a lower duty than similar articles imported from the United Kingdom? It may be suggested with far greater probability that "the friendly feeling on both sides" is more likely to be impaired by the refusal of Her Majesty's Government to relax a Law which imposes an irksome restriction on the fiscal legislation, and vexatiously intermeddles with the domestic taxation, of these self-governed Colonies.

Lord Kimberley seems to complain of the absence of "strong representations and illustrations of the utility or necessity of the measure." The unanimous Resolution of the Conference of last year, and the subsequent identical legislation of New Zealand, South Australia, and Tasmania, may be taken as a sufficient indication of the strength of the conviction of the Governments and Legislatures of Australasia of the urgent necessity, and by consequence in their judgment of the utility, of the measure.

As far as the Colony of Tasmania is concerned, the "necessity and utility of the measure" are sufficiently obvious. Our Customs Duties are imposed for revenue purposes only. But when our nearest neighbours practically close against our producers and manufacturers their best and natural market by the comprehensive operation of an intentionally Protective Tariff, we seek relief in Reciprocity Conventions, which, while they would extend the basis of commercial operations between us and our neighbours, would in no way prejudice the interests of European producers and manufacturers, inasmuch as the desired Convention would, for the most part, "deal with a limited list of raw materials and produce not imported to these Colonies from Europe."

Lord Kimberley's treatment of this question indicates throughout a natural anxiety to avoid a decision which might seem to commit Her Majesty's Government to a departure "from the established commercial policy" of the Mother Country. But, since His Lordship assures us that Her Majesty's Government have not "come to any absolute conclusion on the questions which he has discussed," we may venture to hope that a firm but respectful persistence in the course of legislation already adopted by New Zealand, Tasmania, and South Australia, will shortly secure for the Australasian Colonies that freedom from Imperial restrictions on their fiscal relations with each other which the conciliatory policy of Her Majesty's Government has already conceded to the Colonies of British North America.

JAMES MILNE WILSON.

Colonial Secretary's Office, 11th September, 1871.

His Excellency the Governor.

O

INDEX.

LONDON:
PRINTED BY W. H. SMITH & SON,
186 STRAND.

17—3—75.